Chasing Tornadoes

JESSICA MADDEN

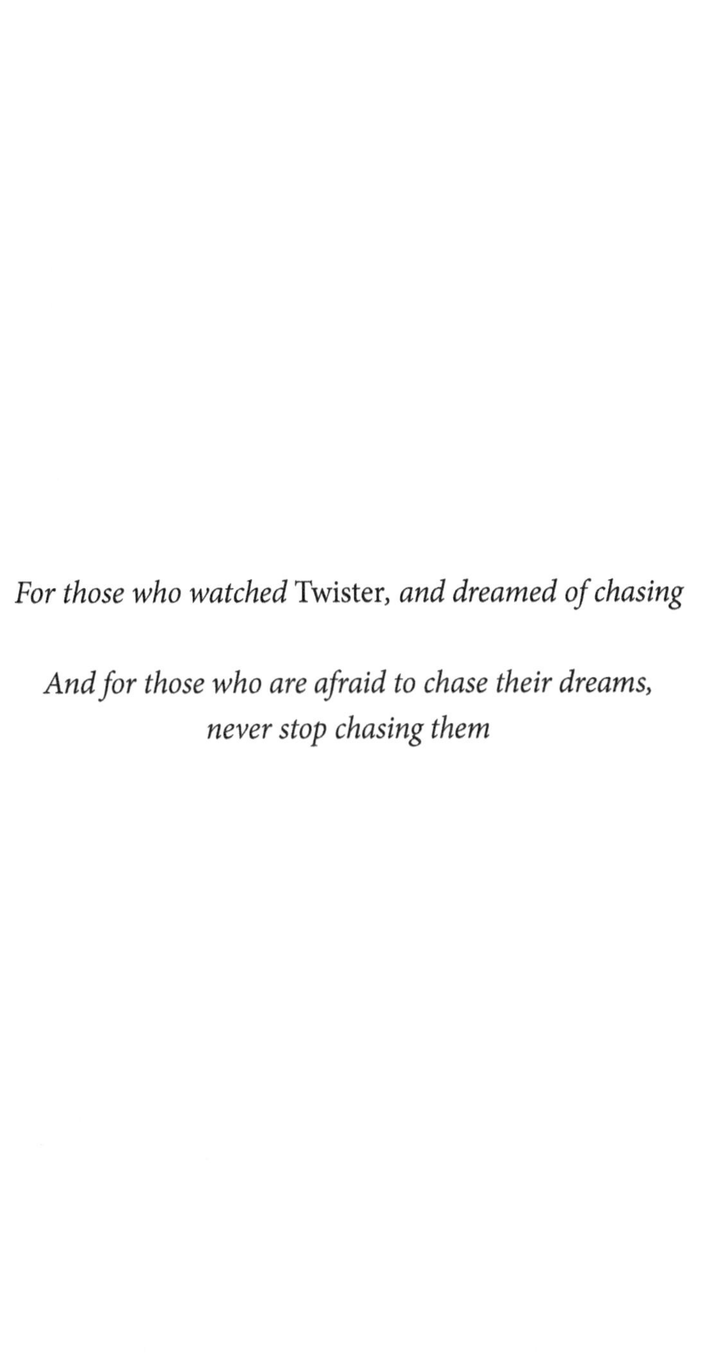

For those who watched Twister, *and dreamed of chasing*

And for those who are afraid to chase their dreams,
never stop chasing them

Prologue

May 7ᵗʰ, 2014

I watch the clouds forming from the living room window. They grow darker by the minute with thunder rumbling in the distance. Mom is listening to the radio as she cooks dinner, the radio announcer talks about the storm forming over Brooke's Creek, Oklahoma. There was a current tornado watch, but the clouds look like it could turn into a warning at any second.

I have never seen a tornado in the ten years I have grown up here in Brooke's Creek. There have been dozens of tornado warnings, the sirens going off to warn people to take shelter, but there has never been one. Not since 1971, when a F4 tornado wiped out the entire town.

My next door neighbor and best friend, Jeremy Hayden, rides into my front yard on his bike. He parks it on the front steps and knocks on the front door. I turn from the window, opening the door.

Jeremy smiles at me when I answered. "Hey, Anna. Do you want to come storm chasing with me?"

Ever since Jeremy and I watched the classic tornado movie *Twister*, Jeremy hasn't been able to stop talking about storm chasing. He has been studying tornadoes and even did a school project on them. They fascinated him and he wanted to know everything about them.

"Now?" I glance over his shoulder at the darkening sky. Was he crazy to be going out in this weather? I turn back to him. "I don't know, Jeremy. It looks like the storm will hit us at any moment."

"Come on, Anna. Please. Just grab your bike so we can watch the clouds. We will take shelter once the storm hits."

Mom joins us at the door. "Oh, hello Jeremy."

Jeremy smiles at her. "Hello, Mrs. Wade. Can Anna come out to play with me for a little while?"

Mom looks at him unsure. "I don't know, Jeremy. The storm looks like it might hit soon. There's also a tornado watch. It might turn to a warning at any second."

"I will keep her safe, Mrs. Wade. Please. Just for a little while? I promise not to go too far from here if any danger occurs."

Mom thinks for a second and then gives in, allowing me to go out with Jeremy for a short time, reminding me to return home or stay in a safe place if the storm worsens. I promise I will. I ran up the stairs to my room to grab my shoes, and then grab my bike from the garage.

We set off down the street, riding our bikes. I had no idea where Jeremy is planning to go, but it wasn't a short distance from our house like he had promised my mother. We ride past the park a few blocks down from where we live, through the main street of Brooke's Creek until we reach the freeway leading out of town. We make our way over to the gas station that's just before the freeway entry.

I keep my eyes on the clouds at all times. There's a hint of green in the darkening clouds. I didn't know much about the weather, but I knew green clouds meant the storm will be severe. We take shelter underneath the gas station just as baseball size hail pelted down. I grip the handlebars on my bike hard until my knuckles turn white. I wanted to go home where I felt safe. Jeremy, on the other hand, was watching the storm with awe. He shows no fear of what the sky planned to do.

When the hail stops, it looked like snow had fallen.

"Jeremy, we should head home," I say to him as thunder rumbles loudly.

"Oh my gosh!" Jeremy says, grabbing my arm. He points to something in the distance across the road in a cornfield. "There's a wall cloud!"

I couldn't follow his excitement. All I wanted was to go home where I could feel safe from the storm. A wall cloud is not what I wanted to feel excited for.

"Jeremy, we need to get home," I tell him, my voice shaking. "If there is going to be a tornado, we should get home and hide in the basement."

I thought he would protest and tell me there was no need to hide from a tornado. I mean, what are the chances a funnel was going to form out of the wall cloud? The majority of tornado warnings we have had in the past ten years were false alarms. But I was thankful Jeremy had agreed with me that we should head back home. The last thing we wanted was to put ourselves at risk or have our parents worry about our whereabouts if something were to happen.

Just as we start pedalling to head back home, Jeremy shouts that a funnel is forming. Fear takes over me as I pedal quickly with Jeremy right behind me. We had to get home. I pray silently to myself that the funnel wouldn't reach the ground. Not until we get home.

We are about ten minutes from our street when the sirens start blaring. Over the siren, thunder rumbles as the storm moves over us. Rain begins pouring, drenching me from head to toe. Once we reach our houses, Jeremy hurries to his home while I head to mine. Mom is standing at the front door, waiting for me. She helps me with my bike, bringing it inside so it's out of the rain. She grabs a towel from the hallway closet, wraps it around me, and together we head downstairs to the basement with my younger brother, Avery, where we take shelter from the storm.

***

A tornado touches down for a brief moment on the outskirts of Brooke's Creek. I don't see Jeremy until the next day when he comes over to talk all enthusiastic about the storm. As much as I didn't share the same enthusiastic feeling he had, I listen to him talk about the storm. He wanted it to be our thing every spring and summer, to go out and storm chase. I told him it was dangerous to do it on our bikes as anything could happen. So we agreed that we would study the clouds and watch the developing storms roll in.

There was never another tornado for any of us to witness after that day. Not until the spring we turned twelve when his Uncle Chris took us storm chasing for the first time. Since then, we chased every storm season, catching a glimpse of tornadoes whenever we could. The summer Jeremy turned sixteen, his parents brought him a car. Together, we would sometimes drive out to storm chase in his car rather than on our bikes. We always kept a distance from the storm.

But two years later on May 3rd, 2022, it was a day I much rather forget.

Chapter 1

May 2nd, 2022

The Day Before

Jeremy texts me in the morning that we are skipping school today. I laugh at his message because I'm already dressed for school. I was going today. We have a math test. A test that was completely pointless and unnecessary as we will be graduating high school in three weeks. But our teacher Mr. Maine didn't care. He wanted us to do a test even if it wasn't going to go towards any grades.

I reply back to his message and reminded him about the test.

Even better to skip school, he replies back.

There is only one reason to why Jeremy wants to skip school today: storm chasing.

We can't skip school to storm chase, I remind him.

Of course we can. Hurry up and get ready. I will be over soon to pick you up.

I shake my head. There is no way I can change Jeremy's mind. He is dead set on going on this chase. Test or no test, he lives for storm chasing. I didn't live for storms like he did, but with my passion for photography, I liked to join him on chases to photograph the storms. One of my pictures even won in a contest last year.

I finish getting ready, and then slip my Canon camera that I got on my second chase, a gift from Jeremy, into my bag. Putting it over my shoulder and head down the stairs. I place my bag beside the door so I can easily pick it up on my way out. Mom hates it when I leave my bag there, claiming it was a tripping hazard, but I made sure it wouldn't be in anyone's way.

I make my way to the kitchen where my parents and brother were. Avery was at the table, eating his cereal. Mom was making herself breakfast, while Dad was drinking the last of his coffee before placing it into the sink.

He turns to Mom as she is buttering toast. "I'm off, Roslyn. I will see you later." He pecks her lips.

"Have a great day at work," Mom says.

Dad moves to my brother next. "See you later, buddy."

He rubs Avery's hair, in which Avery shoos Dad's hand away.

Dad moves over to me. "See you later, Anna. Good luck with your test today." He kisses my forehead.

I give him a small smile. If only he knew I wasn't exactly

sitting down to take it, even when I have spent so much time studying. Hopefully Mr. Maine won't mind Jeremy and I taking the day off today, and let us take the test tomorrow. No doubt Jeremy hasn't studied. I wouldn't be surprise if that's really the reason why he wanted to skip out on the test and the rest of the school to storm chase. Jeremy never liked school, and hated it even more once he became fascinated by storms and all kinds of weather. Why waste a perfectly good day in a classroom when you can be out enjoying it, is what Jeremy always says.

And of course, today was a perfect sunny spring day with warm temperatures reaching up to 80 degrees Fahrenheit.

"Thanks, Dad," I say.

Dad walks out of the kitchen and heads out the front door.

I join my brother at the table, and grab the cereal box he had left for me. He was kind enough to leave a bowl there also, except for the milk, which I had to get from the fridge. I pour it into my bowl. Before I began eating, I glance up at the clock on the microwave. It reads 7:05. Jeremy will be over soon, so I better get a move on with my breakfast. Jeremy is not going to wait for me.

"How do you think you will go with your test?" Mom asks me. She picks up her avocado toast, and sits down across from my brother and I with her plate.

"I'm pretty confident I studied enough," I say. I was mostly a B student. My parents weren't the kind of people who expected me to get an A in all of my classes. No, they just wanted me to try hard and do my best. I was never expecting to get in a top college either. No, my plans after high school were to go to community college and study photography.

Mom gives me a small smile. "I'm sure you will do well,

sweetie."

The front door opens, and it only meant one person: Jeremy. He treated our house like he lived here, and my parents are okay with him helping himself inside as long as he acknowledges himself as he enters.

"Hello?" Jeremy calls out.

"In the kitchen!" I shout out.

"Aw, your boyfriend is here," Avery speaks up, giving me a sneaky smile.

I frown at him. "He's not my boyfriend."

"He should be. He is here every day."

I stick my tongue out at my brother.

"Avery, leave your sister alone," Mom says, who thankfully does not see that I had stuck out my tongue. I expected my brother to rat me out, but he doesn't mention anything to Mom.

Jeremy walks cheerfully into the kitchen. He has on a t-shirt that says 'I'd rather be storm chasing'. He loves wearing it whenever he has the chance to storm chase.

"Good morning," he greets us.

Mom smiles at him. "Good morning, Jeremy. You're nice and cheerful this morning."

Of course he is, Mom, I silently say to myself. *He's skipping school to chase tornadoes today.*

"Yeah, I feel it's going to be a great day," Jeremy explains.

"What's so great about today?" Avery asks. He groans. "We have school. It's never a great day for it."

I quickly eat my cereal, knowing Jeremy isn't going to want to wait for me too long. I have no idea where we are storm chasing today, but Jeremy is the kind of person who likes to head out early to his destination.

Jeremy laughs at my brother's comment. "You got that right."

I eat the last of my cereal, and head to the sink, rinsing the bowl.

I turn to Jeremy. "I'm ready to go."

He smiles. "Sweet." He turns to Mom. "Bye, Mrs. Wade. Have a great day." He turns to my brother. "You have a great day at school, buddy." Jeremy rubs Avery's hair.

Avery pushes his hand away. "Yeah, right."

"You have a good day too, Jeremy," Mom smiles, taking a sip of her coffee.

I stroll over to Mom, hugging her and give her a kiss on the cheek. "See you, Mom."

"See you, Anna. Have a great day at school." She turns to my brother as I pull away. "Avery, hurry up and eat your breakfast so you can get to school."

Jeremy and I leave the kitchen.

He laughs softly so Mom doesn't hear him. "Where we are going is so much better than school."

I grab my school bag and swing it over my shoulder. Then in a low voice so Mom wouldn't hear, "Are you sure you want to skip school?"

"Of course, I'm sure. It's one in a lifetime to see a tornado, and I want to be able to see every one of them." He opens the door and slips out with me close behind him. "I have a very good feeling about this storm system happening over in Kansas this afternoon, and I want to see it."

"Is your uncle coming along?" I ask. His Uncle Chris began going on chases with Jeremy when he said he was interested in it. His uncle took him the summer when we turn twelve. His parents were furious with Chris at first, warning him about getting close to something that was dangerous with their son. But Chris assured them that he kept a distance, and makes sure Jeremy is safe. He has even taken Jeremy's cousin storm chasing a couple of times before taking Jeremy. I have been on a couple of chases with them. There has also been a couple of times Jeremy and I would storm chase together, especially now that he has his own car, but we aren't really allowed to go on a chase without his uncle. Not until we turn eighteen. Jeremy doesn't turn eighteen until next month. Going chasing with his uncle present was a requirement our parents made to ensure our safety until we were older enough to handle the dangerous situations on our own. Jeremy and I have been chasing for six years. We knew the dangers, and we were always careful when we went on our own.

"He's working today," Jeremy unlocks his car that's parked in his driveway, and we hop in. I place my bag in the back seat. He turns to me because he knows I don't like it when we go behind his uncle's back without him on a chase. "Everything will be fine, Anna. Trust me, this is something so much better than some stupid math test. One we don't even need to do when we are graduating in three weeks. We can do it tomorrow."

I nod, slipping on my seat belt. "So, how are we getting out of school without our parents knowing we had skipped school?"

We have only ever skipped school twice this tornado season to storm chase. Both of them without Chris.

Jeremy's lips curl into a sneaky smile. "Do you even have to ask?"

Of course, I didn't have to because we knew the perfect person to cover for us.

I pull out my phone and call our friend Moxie.

"Hey, Moxie," I greet her as soon as she answers.

"Hey, Anna."

I had my phone on speaker and Jeremy announces himself.

"Hey, Moxie, Jeremy and I have a favor to ask," I say.

I didn't have to ask. She knew what I wanted.

"Sure, I can phone the school for you."

Moxie is an actress, and was able to change the sound of her voice to anything you ask her to do. To imitate our mothers, she was able to put on a voice that would sound different, and you would never take notice she is the same person on the phone. I honestly believe she will make an excellent voice actor someday.

"Thanks, Moxie," Jeremy says. "We owe you."

"You guys stay safe, okay?" Moxie tells us. "Where are you headed?"

I turn to Jeremy, unsure where he was taking us. He had said we will be going to Kansas, but I wasn't sure where we were going exactly.

"We are headed to Kansas," Jeremy explains. "There's a huge storm system predicted to head there later this afternoon."

"Okay, well I will talk to you later and you can tell me all about your day."

I hang up and slip the phone back into my pocket.

"Ready?" Jeremy asks me, smiling as he turns the ignition.

I return the smile. "Ready."

Chapter 2

The Kansas/Oklahoma border is an hour and a half from Brooke's Creek. The place Jeremy was driving us to is Meadow Ridge, an hour from the border, making the drive two hours and half. I like the long drives, the feeling of being on the open road and being free.

We take short breaks to stop for toilet breaks and food, grabbing something from the gas station when Jeremy fills up his car. He also stops on the side of the road to admire the clouds. In the distance you could see the clouds building up for the afternoon storms predicted, white and fluffy.

We reach Meadow Ridge by noon. The storm still hasn't form. We stop at a park so Jeremy could study up the radar and look at reports to where the storm cell will be, and where a twister was more likely to form. Maybe it won't be out here in Meadow Ridge, but another town over. Meanwhile he did that, I took photographs of the sky with the incredible cloud formations in the distance.

"I think we might have to move north east," Jeremy says, closing his laptop. "This morning I thought it would hit around here, but what I see on the radar, north east is where it seems tornadoes could form."

One of the things I hated about storm chasing is the guess work to where a tornado is more likely to form. Some supercells produce tornadoes, and there are others that don't. I only hope that Jeremy's prediction was worth skipping school. But even if we don't see a tornado, at least I get to be out here with my best friend. I also get awesome photos of the sky. Photographing storms is what I enjoy. After high school, Jeremy really wants me to continue being his storm chasing partner. I may not be as passionate with storm chasing like he is, but I wouldn't miss being his partner. He has even suggested I sell some of the photos I have taken to magazines and other media. I haven't done that yet, but maybe someday I will.

"Any tornado watches?" I ask.

Jeremy nods. "Yes, there's a tornado watch in the whole of Glenfield County."

"Is Meadow Ridge in Glenfield County?"

"Yes, just on the outskirts of it. I reckon this storm will hit bad in the centre of the county."

I stare up at the sky, watching the clouds in the distance. Unlike Jeremy, I can't read the radar, so I honestly have no idea where the storm will most likely develop. I trust him to know where the storm will hit, and for him to keep us safe. Whether we see a tornado or not today, we will be home late and our parents will kill us for going chasing on our own.

"Okay," I say, getting off the table I'm sitting on in the park. "Let's get something to eat before we head off. I will also check in with Moxie."

I message Moxie once we get into the car, and Jeremy drives to the gas station to grab something for lunch. Moxie informs me that everything went smoothly when she pretended to be Jeremy's and my mother when she rang the school. It is unclear to when we will get back to Brooke's Creek, but I told her I will text my mother later to say I will be at her place. She didn't reply back, but I figured she was probably back in class.

While Jeremy waits in the car, I buy us a sandwich inside. We eat it quickly before heading northeast.

Brighton is the town we decided to stop at and storm watch. Here, the clouds were beginning to darken. It is just after one thirty. Thunder rumbles in the distance. There are several other storm chasers parked on the side of the road also.

Jeremy and I stand on the side of the road near a farm, looking out on a field to where the dark clouds were. I take out my camera and snap a few pictures. I look over him a few times, watching Jeremy as he studies the approaching storm, wondering what it was going to do. When it came to the weather, he always paid attention to the sky. It fascinated him, and being able to chase them is what drew his passion for storms even more. He wanted to get close and experience the power.

Some chasers began to get back into their cars. Jeremy decides to do the same. Before we drive off, Jeremy checks the radar again, choosing the path to take. He searches for a hook echo on the radar, anything to tell us what location we should get to and view the storm. But nothing showed up yet.

Jeremy heads to the south, just a few minutes outside

of Brighton. When we get to the location, the clouds have darkened even more, making it feel like it was dusk. The storm was building up, and I keep an eye out for a wall cloud or funnel. There's a moment where I'm unsure what the storm is going to do, and want to get back into the vehicle where I felt safe, especially with the lightning flashing across the sky. But I try not to focus on the terrifying part of the storm, and focus on the beauty of the clouds formation. The way the clouds moved across the sky calms me.

I'm busy capturing the sky when Jeremy grabs my arm, and points to the northeast.

"Anna! Look! A wall cloud!" he excitedly says.

I follow his direction and see the wall cloud across the field. My eyes light up knowing that this could be it. The storm could produce a tornado. It's what we came to see. I take a few pictures of it.

Jeremy pulls me in the direction of his car. "Come on, let's get closer."

We drive closer in the direction of the wall cloud. Not too close because we didn't want to get into the core in case the storm drops baseball size hail or if a funnel drops, it becomes rain wrapped. It begins to rain as we move down the road. Jeremy keeps is eyes on both the road and the wall cloud, checking for any signs if a funnel cloud drops. I do the same. I also film it on his phone.

Jeremy pulls over and gets out of the car while I stay inside. He uses his drone to scan the area, and to get a view of the storm from above. I spot a glimpse of green in the clouds. I remember when I was a kid I was always terrified of green clouds, knowing it meant severe weather. Now when I see them, it only scares me slightly, bringing on an adrenaline rush, wondering what the storm is going to do.

It's almost two o'clock. School was letting out in an hour, so I quickly message my mom to let her know that I will be at Moxie's before I didn't get a chance to do it later. I slip in Jeremy's name too, just in case he doesn't message his parents of his whereabouts, and I don't want his parents wondering where he is. I wanted my mom to at least know where I could be before we lose signal on our phones. I hated lying to my mom about my whereabouts, but I knew how furious she and Dad will be if they find out where we truly are. They are okay with me going storm chasing, but only if Jeremy's uncle is with us to ensure my safety.

Jeremy hops back into the car. He puts his seat belt on. "There's some rotation in that wall cloud. It's definitely going to produce a tornado."

At the mention of it, the radio station we are listening to issues a tornado warning.

"Should we stay here or should we move position?" I ask, glancing over at the wall cloud to our left. A funnel cloud might drop any second.

Jeremy looks out the windshield. "Let's move away from here and go further up the road."

We move a little further up the road. As Jeremy drives, I keep an eye on the wall cloud, watching the clouds rotate. It has only been a few minutes when I spot a funnel cloud.

"Jeremy, a funnel!" I point out.

Jeremy looks in the direction, and then pulls to the side of the road. He grabs his phone and films the funnel cloud.

"Oh my gosh, it's incredible!" Jeremy shouts excitedly.

I use my own phone to call in to report the funnel. A few seconds after I called it in, the sirens began wailing in the town.

We stand there, watching the funnel cloud until it reaches the ground, sweeping up dirt in the field. It starts moving, heading towards houses in the rural area of Brighton, a direct path to the town. My heart beats fast, praying silently it won't cause too much damage to the town.

Getting back into the car, we race alongside it, the adrenaline pumping. Jeremy makes sure he doesn't get too close to the whirlwind, not wanting debris to hit us.

It narrowly misses a home, and keeps going. I snap a few photographs of the tornado and also help Jeremy film it. The tornado looks spectacular through the lenses, ripping up a barn. It always fascinated me on how it moves and tearing structures apart. Beside me, Jeremy tells me excitedly what a beauty this tornado is.

We follow the twister as it moves across the rural area before moving into the small town of Brighton.

Jeremy turns onto a street that is running parallel to the tornado. We can't see the tornado, just the top of the funnel cloud as we passed buildings that block our view. I begin to notice the debris falling near us. My heart is caught in my throat, realizing the danger we are in. If the debris is hitting us, it meant we were too close, and with the limited visual we had, the last thing we needed was the tornado catching us off guard and come towards us.

"Jeremy, I think you need to pull back a bit," I say. "We are getting hit by debris. We are too close."

Jeremy doesn't show any kind of fear of being too close. He tells me are fine.

"Jeremy, back up," I demand. "We are too close."

We stop at an intersection; the traffic lights are out as they sway in the wind. There are still people out on the street, driving, unsure which way to go with the tornado. Jeremy and I sit at the lights for a moment and watch the tornado. Jeremy has his window down of his Toyota Camry, and all you can hear is the roaring wind coming from the tornado as it tears apart everything in its path. The sound of it was enough to leave you shaking with fear.

Continuing on, we keep up with the tornado until it leaves the town and moves into more rural areas. We stop the car for a bit, filming it. Even when we are at a distance, the wind was still mighty powerful, like it would sweep us both. The tornado is on the ground for fifteen minutes before roping out.

***

"Aren't you glad we skip school today?" Jeremy asks me where as we sit on the hood of his car on the side of the road after the tornado has dissipated. There's still a bit of thunder as the storm moves on. Hopefully this supercell doesn't produce another tornado somewhere else.

In the distance we can hear sirens from emergency vehicles. Often when we storm chase, we go to help anyone who needs help, but today we can't do that if we want to get back home before our parents find out where we are. After following the tornado through the town, we wanted to take a bit of a break before we head south back to Brooke's Creek, Oklahoma. Now that the storm has past, there's a break in the clouds where blue skies were beginning to appear. It was like there was never a destructive tornado on the ground.

"While I rather be in school," I say, "it was still fun to be out here with you."

"Are you able to come storm chasing with my uncle and I

this summer?"

I was able to storm chase with Jeremy and his uncle last summer when he first started to storm chase in his new car. It was fun, but this summer I wasn't sure. Avery has started baseball this year, so I will be attending his games. Also, I wanted to spend this summer preparing for college. I was attending community college in the fall, one that was close to home and I didn't have to worry about moving halfway across the country. I also plan to build up a portfolio for my pictures to share with job interviews and internships.

"I might," I answer. Jeremy and his uncle will storm chase in June, the last month of storm chasing season, so maybe I could chase on some days. "It all depends on Avery's games. I also want to focus on building up my portfolio."

Jeremy smiles at me. "Which is exactly why you should come storm chasing with Uncle Chris and I this summer."

I raise my eyebrow at him. "Really?"

"Okay, so not only did I want to skip school and storm chase today, but I really wanted you out here with me, Anna. There's something I want to tell you, and I thought this chase would be perfect to share the news. My uncle is inviting my cousins to come chase with us. They are in their first year of college, studying meteorology. He thought it would be great to chase with them. We have never chased all together before."

I have met a few of Jeremy's cousins, and I know Chris didn't have a partner or any kids.

"Which cousins are joining us?" I want to know.

"Jonah and Lindy."

I have a brief memory of Jonah and Lindy. Jeremy once invited me along to his aunt's wedding when she got remarried. Lindy is Jonah's stepbrother.

"I don't know, Jeremy." I have always just chased with the two of them, and never with anyone else. I can't imagine chasing with anyone other than Jeremy and Chris.

"I know you might not want to go chasing with other people, but since you are thinking to build up your portfolio this summer, why not do it during the chase? Anna, think of all the amazing photos you can build up the portfolio you want for internships and job interviews. Not only storms, but we will be out on the road, and you can take amazing pictures of the landscape or whatever pictures you want to take." His face lit up. "The best part is Uncle Chris is going to allow us to get up close to a tornado as part of research Lindy and Jonah are doing. This is my chance to get up really close to one, and I want you to experience it with me."

I think about what he says, and he is right. This will be an amazing opportunity to work on my photography portfolio for future employment. But then a spark of fear washes over me at the thought of getting up close to an actual tornado. I enjoy viewing them from the distance, but to get up to one as part of research his cousins are doing, was that even safe? What if something goes wrong?

I want to say no. Viewing them from the distance was one thing, but being up close to one was another. Jeremy had always spoke to me about becoming a meteorologist, and intercept them for science. That thought terrified me. I like photographing storms, not studying the science side of it. But Jeremy really wanted me to come along, and I couldn't let him down.

"Okay." I nod with a smile. "I will tag along with you."

Jeremy smiles brightly and then hugs me. "I can't wait to spend this summer with you. I swear it's going to be even better than last summer. I just know we are going to have an awesome storm chasing season."

"So, do you know when we are going to start chasing with your cousins?" I ask.

"Once school breaks out for summer at the end of the month."

"Awesome."

I glance at my phone to check the time. It's almost four o'clock.

"We better get home, Jeremy. We have a long drive back, and we don't want our parents to start worrying about our whereabouts." I slip my phone into my pocket.

Jeremy nods. "You're right. But before we head back, let's take a photo to remember this day."

He puts his arm around my waist, pulling me closer to him. We smile into the camera and he snaps a photo of us.

"I will send you the picture as soon as we get home. Thanks for coming out here with me today, Anna."

Getting into the car, it takes us a while to get out of Brighton, trying to get around the destruction the tornado had left behind. Even though we weren't going to help anyone out so we could get back home in time, we drove a couple of injured people to the hospital.

We make it home just after six. I message Moxie to let her know we had made it back safely.

Before I got to bed, Jeremy sends me the photo of us that we had taken. I smile at it and save it to my phone, making it my background.

Chapter 3

May 3rd, 2022

Jeremy comes over in the morning. He strolls into the kitchen where my brother and I are eating our breakfast. Mom stands at the island, preparing a peanut butter and jelly sandwich for my brother's lunch.

"Good morning, everyone," he greets us all.

I look up from where I am reading over my notes for my math test, hoping Mr. Maine wouldn't be mad that Jeremy and I wasn't at school yesterday to do it. When my parents had asked me about the test, I told them that we didn't do the test and it will be today. I wave to Jeremy, and turn back to my notes.

"Good morning, Jeremy," Avery returns the greeting.

Mom looks up from the island and smiles. "Morning, Jeremy."

He sits down at the table across from me. "How's it going, Anna?"

I don't look up at him as I keep my eyes focus on the notes. "I'm good."

He waves his hand over my book to get my attention. I look up at him, frowning.

"Do you mind? I'm trying to study."

Jeremy sits up. "What for? We have our final grades already. It's not like it will matter if you fail this dumb test Mr. Maine is getting us to do."

I close my book. "I know, but still, I would like to do well."

Jeremy doesn't respond. Instead, he says, "Ready to go?"

I raise an eyebrow at him. "Wow, someone is eager to get to school."

I stand up, picking up my book. I walk over to the island where Mom is, grabbing an apple from the fruit bowl.

Jeremy chuckles, standing up also. "Trust me, but I'm not that eager to get to school. Honestly, I want to skip school altogether and go storm chasing with my uncle today. There's going to be a storm this afternoon in our county. There's a prediction it could produce multiple tornadoes."

"Well, let's hope there won't be." I turn to Mom. "I'm going to head off."

Mom smiles. "Okay, sweetie. You have a great day at school." She kisses my cheek.

I turn to my brother. "Bye, Avery."

"Bye," my brother says with his mouth full.

Before I leave the kitchen, Mom stops me. "Are you still

able to pick your brother up from baseball practice this afternoon?"

I nod. "I can do it."

"Thanks, sweetie. I will see you later."

Jeremy and I escape before my mother could call me back. I grab my bag near the front door, swinging it over my shoulder and walk out with Jeremy. We headed down the lawn towards his car.

"I wish you could come storm chasing today," Jeremy tells me.

"I know. I would like to, but neither of my parents can pick Avery up, so I have to do it."

"I was talking to my uncle last night about the supercells that will be over Oklahoma. The storm looks like it will hit Brooke's Creek. Are you alright with getting home yourself this afternoon?"

A wave of fear rushes over me at the thought of the storm Jeremy had talked about producing multiple tornadoes that could hit our town. I have storm chased with Jeremy and his uncle so many times, capturing tornadoes from the distance. They look so fascinating out there when they are in the middle of nowhere, away from anything they can destroy. But when they start moving towards towns and metropolitan areas, it's the most terrifying thing ever. Jeremy and I have never been up close to a tornado. His Uncle Chris doesn't allow us to get too close. I just don't want to imagine the vortex moving towards our town, destroying everything I have ever known.

But then I quickly let go of that fear because most likely the tornado will miss us like it has done every year. Three out of four tornado warnings are false, and this one will most likely be false as well.

"I should be okay," I say. "I will probably hang out in the library before heading to Avery's school to pick him up from baseball practice."

"Maybe Moxie will be able to give you a lift." He unlocks the car, and we hop in.

"No, she is starting her job at the grocery store today." I put on my seat belt.

"Oh right. I completely forgot." He turns the ignition and then put on his seat belt.

"How did you forget when she has been talking about it non-stop all week?"

Jeremy shrugs. "It completely slipped my mind. Come on, let's get to school."

He shifts the gear into reverse and backs out of the driveway.

* * *

Moxie fills us in on what we had missed out in school yesterday. Turns out Mr. Maine was off, so none of our classmates did the test. He was still off today, and I was thankful I didn't have to stress over it. We were graduating soon, so it wasn't like this test was going to be part of our final grade. Mr. Maine just likes to torture us with his tests, even if it's completely unnecessary.

By midday, there were fluffy white clouds building up in the distance. It was too early to tell what Mother Nature has in store for us this afternoon, but the warm spring air made it the perfect ingredient for the stormy weather. I only hope that we are just getting a thunderstorm and not a tornado.

With the nice weather, Moxie and I decided to eat lunch outside. Jeremy was off taking a phone call with his Uncle

Chris about this afternoon and promised to join us as soon as he is finished with the call.

"Do you think we will get a tornado?" I ask Moxie, biting into my tuna salad sandwich.

Moxie shrugs, stabbing a fork into her salad. "Who knows? I mean, how many times over the years did they say we will get a tornado, they set off the sirens and then turns out it was all just a false alarm?" She put what she had on her fork into her mouth.

"True, but I guess in a way it's better to be safe than sorry. Jeremy is definitely sure there is going to be a tornado."

"He always says that, anything for his thrill-seeking adventures. I'm not sure how you guys can be so game to go storm chasing. The thought of it makes me want to run in the other direction."

I laugh. "Storm chasing isn't too bad. Yes, it's terrifying, especially when tornadoes are unpredictable, but fun." Honestly, I probably wouldn't have gotten into chasing if it wasn't for Jeremy. Tornadoes terrified me, but photographing storms is what I enjoy doing. I would either not be into photography, or I would be taking photos of storms from my backyard if Jeremy never invited me out to chase, but that isn't the same as getting out on the road to find storms.

Moxie points her fork at me. "I swear you two are made for each other. How aren't you guys dating?"

This is the first time Moxie has ever said this to me, and it surprises me. I hear it from my brother, telling me he should be my boyfriend, but it's the first time from my friend. Jeremy and I have been friends and neighbors for so long that we never even thought of becoming more. I don't even see each other more than that.

"We are just friends, Moxie," I tell her.

"You should totally give dating a go with him. You and Jeremy will be perfect for each other."

I shake my head. "I don't see him as any more than that."

Jeremy chooses the perfect moment to come over, ending the conversation Moxie and I were having as he takes a seat next to me. "Hello, ladies."

"Hello, Jeremy," I answer, ignoring Moxie staring at me. I still couldn't believe she thinks Jeremy and I should be more than friends. "So, you and your uncle are all set for this afternoon?"

Jeremy nods, picking up the other half of my sandwich. "All set. I'm meeting him over in Plainville, where he feels the storm will likely develop." He bites into it.

"Hey!" I cry. "That's my mine!"

Jeremy gives me a cheeky smile. "And it's delicious too. Thanks."

I playfully narrow my eyes at him. "Dweeb."

Jeremy sticks out his tongue, giving me a disgusting view of mashed up bread and tuna salad.

I glance over at Moxie, and she gives me a look that says 'See, you guys are perfect for each other.' I ignore her look.

"So, my uncle reckons the storm could hit just around 3:00 this afternoon. I'm meeting up with him as soon as school ends at three. Hopefully we can get out earlier." He looks over at me. "Are you sure you will be fine with getting home, Anna?"

I nod, reaching for my bottle of water. "I will be alright. Like I said, I'm going to hang out at the library before heading to my brother's school once he is finished with baseball practice."

"I wish I could stay back and then drive you later," Moxie

says as I unscrew the lid with one hand while holding onto the other half of the sandwich.

"No need to apologize, Moxie. I know how it's important that you are starting that new job."

"Oh yes, good luck with it today," Jeremy says, stuffing the rest of my sandwich into his mouth.

"Thanks," Moxie says. She turns to me. "I hope you don't get caught in the storm."

Jeremy turns to me, tilting his head. "Make sure you stay close to shelter, Anna. Uncle Chris is pretty sure this this storm will produce a tornado."

I thank Jeremy for his concern, and promise him I will keep close to shelter. But I'm sure I will be okay. There wasn't going to be a tornado.

Chapter 4

The clouds in the distance were getting darker by the end of the day as they approach closer to our town. I didn't have any classes with Jeremy for the last two classes of the day, but I can imagine him staring out the windows. He would be paying little attention to whatever his teacher is saying, getting excited for the storm chase he has planned later this afternoon.

At 2:00, our principal Mrs. Dawson announces over the P.A. that she was dismissing us an hour early, giving us enough time to get home before the storm hits. We were under a tornado watch, but according to the clouds forming outside, it could change to a warning at any moment. An alert had gone out to all schools in our county for us to be let out early. We do have a storm shelter in our school just in case, but I guess the National Weather Service just wants everyone to be prepared.

Moxie, Jeremy and I walk out of the school together. School buses were out front, and parents were also at the school picking up their kids. It was like it was already the end of the school day.

"Are you alright with getting to your brother's school?" Moxie asks me. "I don't mind driving you."

I glance up at the clouds that are moving fast into our town. I turn back to Moxie. "I should be fine. You go and get ready for your new job."

Moxie doesn't look convinced as she stares at me with a concern look. "We are under a tornado watch, Anna. Plus, the elementary school is twenty blocks from here. What if a tornado does come and you can't find shelter?"

I watch the clouds. Sure, a tornado is unpredictable, and the last thing I wanted was to be stuck somewhere without shelter. But there wasn't anything to worry about. We weren't getting a tornado. If we do, it was going to bypass our town like it has done every year since it struck our town in 1971. I will be safe walking to my brother's school.

"I will be fine," I answer. "Everything is going to be fine."

It was Jeremy's turn to be concerned now. "Moxie's right, Anna. By the look of those clouds, we are definitely getting a severe storm. There is no doubt in my mind that a tornado will form."

I put a hand on both of my friends' shoulders. "I will be fine, guys. Really. I promise you. I will find shelter if the worst happens."

Moxie nods. "Okay. You be safe, Anna." She gives me a hug.

"Same goes to you. I hope everything goes well with your new job."

"Thanks," she says as she pulls away. "That's if I get to work.

If there really is a tornado coming, we might not work."

"I'm sure everything will be fine," Jeremy says, hugging her before she heads off to her car. "Have fun, Moxie."

Once she is gone, Jeremy turns to me. His brown eyes filled with worry even when I told him I was going to be fine. We have had many tornado watches in the past that did turn in a warning, and nothing happened. There wasn't a tornado then, and there wasn't going to be one today.

"Jeremy, I mean it. You don't need to worry about me. I'm going to be fine."

"I just want to make sure you're safe."

I give him a small smile. "I know, and I'm going to be. Why don't you head out and meet your uncle? You don't want to miss anything."

Jeremy hugs me. "I will call you later. Be safe, Anna."

"Bye Jeremy."

He pulls away from me and I watch him as he walks to his car. I think about what Moxie had said earlier at lunch. I'm not sure how she ever thought we would make a great couple. We only saw each other as friends. Dating wasn't exactly something I was interested in right now.

My thoughts are interrupted when my phone rings, and I turn my eyes from Jeremy. I fish my phone out of my pocket. It's my mother calling.

"Hi, Mom," I say.

"Hey, sweetie. Did your school get dismissed early?" she asks.

I nod. "Yes, we did. I'm currently at the front of the school."

"Great. Avery's school was also dismissed. Your father and I aren't able to pick him up. His baseball practice is cancelled because of the storm. Could you go and pick him up?"

"Sure. No problems, Mom."

"Thanks, Anna. Be safe, okay?"

"I will, Mom."

I hang up. I look over to where Jeremy had parked his car this morning only to see he had already left. I glance up at the sky, studying the clouds. It was so hard to know what this storm is going to do, and I only hope I can get to my brother's school in time. Maybe I should've taken Moxie's offer and get a lift from her.

But when I go to find Moxie, she has already left the school.

I guess I just have to hope I get to the school in time.

I head to Brooke's Creek Elementary, taking my time. It's about a half an hour walk. I keep an eye on the clouds as I walk, noticing green in them. Maybe I should start picking up my pace. Green clouds are never a good thing. It doesn't necessarily mean a tornado, but hail could fall and I don't exactly have anything to protect myself from the hail stones, except maybe my bag that I could use to cover my head with.

Thunder rumbles loudly in the distance. The storm is getting closer. I'm about three streets away from the school when my phone alerts me with a message. I stop for a moment, taking it out to find that there is a tornado warning issue for our area. I look up at the sky, studying the clouds as they move fast. If there's a tornado warn message, then it would be best to make a run for the rest of the way to Avery's school.

I pull up the radar to see where this storm is at. Jeremy had mentioned earlier that the storm was predicted to hit us around 3:00. It is now 2:38.

It beings to rain. Great. I don't even have my umbrella with me.

I start walking again when my phone rings. I pull it out to

find it's Jeremy.

"Hey, Jeremy."

"Anna, are you at your brother's school yet?" he wants to know, his voice fill with concern.

"I'm almost there."

"Hurry, Anna! I'm over in Plainville. A tornado is on the ground, nearing the freeway into town. You have maybe ten minutes before it hits Brooke's Creek. It's big. It's a wedge tornado! It's violent, and oh gosh, Anna, from the damage I'm seeing, it could be an EF4 or EF5."

The tornado sirens began blaring. My heart beats fast knowing the danger I'm currently in by being out on the street. I have at least thirteen minutes to seek shelter at my brother's school, maybe less. Plainville is the next town over to us. It won't take long for the twister to get here.

I hang up the phone and race to my brother's school. By the time I reach the elementary school, I'm about to collapse. My lungs are burning, my legs can't run anymore, but there's no time to rest.

And then I see it. In the distance from the east of the school is the large wedge tornado Jeremy had warned me about. My mouth gapes opened at the sight of it. I have never seen a tornado that huge before. I haven't seen the damage path yet, but Jeremy is right. This tornado is going to be violent.

I honestly thought Jeremy was bluffing when he said the tornado was to hit Brooke's Creek. I never thought we would ever get another one after the 1971 one.

I have no idea how far the tornado is from me. The wind is strong and I can hear the roaring wind from the twister. I watch as shingles from roofs are lifted of buildings, before larger parts are broken up and circle around the rotating column of air. In the distance it looks like it's standing still, and that's when I knew it's heading in my direction.

I race to the school and swing open the doors. The hallway is empty, and I don't see anyone. There are cars in the staff parking lot, so I knew the teachers were still here. They must be in the storm shelter. The problem is I had no idea where the storm shelter in Avery's school is.

"Avery!" I scream my brother's name as I run down the corridor.

I find the map of the school near the administration office. I quickly scan it, to see what their evacuation plan is and where the storm shelter is located. I find it in the back of the school building.

I make my way down there. I needed to get to my brother. I have to make sure he is safe.

I'm so focus with getting to the shelter, that I don't even glance outside when I passed the windows in the corridor. Not until a branch from a tree crash through a window. It narrowly misses me, and I cover my face to avoid the glass. The roaring freight train noise is loud, like it was getting closer. I turn to my left, glancing out the window the branch had flown through, and there it is. The tornado is right across the street from the school.

That's when I realize I'm going to die. I'm not going to get to the storm shelter in time. If I had taken Moxie's offer of giving me a lift here, I would have been safe. But I thought I could make it by walking.

Now death was right near me, and I had only seconds to take cover.

There was no point running to the other side of the school where the shelter is. The tornado will be here before I get to it. So I take cover in the restroom that is near me. I hid in a stall, closing the door, and crotch down into the tornado safety position I had always been taught in school, never having to use it until now.

The lights in the restroom flicker before sending the room into complete darkness. With the lights off, it made it even scarier as the tornado approaches. My ears pop as the air pressure drops. The roaring of the wind as well as all sorts of debris hitting against the building or glass shattering. I hear things breaking and I have no idea where the sounds are coming from.

And then there's an even louder smash as something big rips through the building. I squeeze my eyes shut as the roof is ripped off, afraid to open my eyes to see what's happening. The door to the bathroom is blown open. Everything around me is so loud that I can't even hear myself screaming.

I sneak a peek to see what's happening, looking up above me to where the ceiling used to be. The tornado is right on top of me, debris flying everywhere, beams falling from the ceiling.

Something hits the wall behind the stall I'm in, and the wall started to crumble. I need to get out of here before it crushes me.

Getting to my feet, I move out of the stall in time as the wall crumbles down right where I was crouched. Something whizzes past me, knocking me to the tile floor, my knees hitting the tiles hard. Another object struck the side of my cheek. I let out a cry before crouching under the sink. I hold onto the pipe, afraid of being swept up by the wind.

Then within seconds, the tornado is gone.

Chapter 5

Everything is silent once the tornado passes, except for the wind as the tornado moves on.

I sit there for a moment under the sink, too terrified to move. I have storm chased with Jeremy and his uncle so many times, watching these whirlwinds from the distance. But never have I been in an actual tornado. I felt for the people who have gone through this from the chases I have been on, and I wasn't sure how I have survived just then.

Scattered around the restroom floor were all sorts of debris – papers, torn books, wood, bricks, pieces of the ceiling.

I was so glad I had gotten to my brother's school in time. I don't know what I would do if I wasn't near it. Maybe try to seek shelter in someone's home in hope they would let me be in their basement or storm cellar? The wall for the stall I was in had completely crumble in. A steel beam had gone through the crumble wall, right where I had been. If I hadn't moved when I did, I would have been trapped underneath there. Or worse, I could be dead.

Rain comes in. I glance up at the sky, the roof completely gone.

I carefully get off the floor, and catch a glimpse of my face in the cracked, muddy mirror. Whatever sharp thing that scrape my cheek, there's a cut there and blood is pouring out of it. But other than the wound on my face, I was completely uninjured.

Carefully walking over the pile of rubble, I make my way to the corridor of the school. The restroom door has come off, and I glance into the hallway and gasp.

One side of the corridor that looked out onto the street and car park was gone. A few classrooms remain standing, but the roof had completely caved in. Stepping out was almost if I was suddenly in a war zone and not the aftermath of a tornado. If I had stayed in the corridor, I would have definitely been killed. I still don't even know how I survived, but I'm thankful I'm still breathing.

I pull out my phone in hope to hear from Jeremy, but there's no cell service. I put my phone back in my pocket.

I hear voices. Someone telling others to follow him. I glance down the corridor to where the tornado shelter would be, seeing the school principal walking down, carefully stepping over the rubble. With him is a few students whose parents haven't had the chance to pick them up early. There are a few staff members with the children also, trying their best to keep them calm while they hide their own fears in their voices.

Amongst the children is my brother.

As soon as I see him, I burst into tears.

"Avery!" my voice chokes as I make my way towards him.

Avery glances my way. He has his school bag with him. Pushing past the other students, he makes his way over to me.

"Anna!"

I reach my brother and scoop him into my arms. We cry into each other's shoulders.

"I was so scared, Anna," he tells me.

"I know, buddy," I say as I pull away from him, wiping my tears. "I was too."

"I wish you were here with me. I was hoping you would come, but you didn't make it."

I rest my hands on his shoulders. I examine him to see he had no injuries on him. "I know. I got here as soon as the tornado hit. I took shelter in the restroom."

He reaches up to touch my cheek, but doesn't touch the blood. "You're bleeding, Anna."

"I know." I take his hand. "I'm okay."

A teacher comes over to us.

"Are you hurt, honey?" she asks me.

"I'm fine. Something cut my face, but I'm okay."

The teacher gestures to where there's a hole in a wall of what used to be a classroom. The students and other teachers were walking out of it.

"Let's get you two out of here." She points to the roof. "This roof could collapse at any second."

We follow the teacher through the hole and join the others outside.

I have seen damage from tornadoes many times on chases, but when you see the damage in your own backyard, everything you once knew is completely gone in seconds.

A few buildings were left standing, but many had half of the walls down with no roof, or they were completely reduced to rubble. Many trees were uprooted or strip bare. I was sure I was having some kind of nightmare, but all of this was too real to be one. I wanted to kick myself for not taking Jeremy seriously when he said there will be a high chance of tornadoes. I wanted to believe that one wasn't going to come to our town again after the 1971 one.

The rain has slowed down, and where I stand with my brother in what used to be the car park, now is just a pile of turned over cars and other pieces of twisted debris. I look around at my surroundings. Nothing is familiar anymore. It was like we were toss into a whole new world.

Avery squeezes my hand tightly. "Anna, I'm scared."

I turn to him, getting down to his level. "Hey, it's okay. I'm here now."

"Is the tornado going to come back?" He chokes on a sob.

I glance up at the sky where it remains grey and the rain falls, hitting me in the face. I wipe away the water from my face as I turn back to my brother. "No, it's not going to come back. It's gone now. We are safe, Avery."

"I want Mom and Dad."

"We will find them. Let's get home and hopefully they will be there."

Avery nods, wiping his eyes and sniffing.

Standing up and taking my brother's hand, we begin walking in the direction of our home, unsure if it will be still standing.

We walk along the road. There are people screaming, crying or calling for help as they emerge from the rubble and pick through their ruined homes. I almost got lost trying to find our street because nothing was recognizable, even though I had walked these streets so many times.

The whole walk home was silent, and the whole time I'm trying to prepare myself and my brother that we may not be coming home to a house. For all we know, the tornado probably destroyed it, like it did with everything else in its path.

As we reach the front yard, there's some debris there, and a few smash windows. But other than that, our house was untouched. Jeremy's house was also untouched.

Jeremy. I hope he is okay. I look up and down the street, expecting him to pull in at any second to see how I was, and to tell me all about the chase.

Instead of seeing Jeremy's car, we see our mother's. She had just gotten home and was getting out of the car.

"Mommy!" Avery cries out.

He let's go of my hand and runs across the lawn towards our mother.

"Oh, thank goodness," she cries, opening her arms and pulls Avery into them. "I'm so glad you're safe."

"I was so scared."

"I know, baby. I know."

I reach my mom and she pull me into a hug. The three of us stand there for a moment, not leaving each other's arms.

"Have you heard from Dad?" I ask mom.

She pulls away. "Not since before the storm hit. He's still at work, and will be on his way home soon. Did you get to the elementary school alright?" She puts a hand on my cheek. "Are you hurt, Anna?"

I try not to think about what could have happened if I hadn't made it in time.

"I got there just as the tornado hit. I took shelter in the bathroom at the school. And I'm okay. I just had something sharp cut me."

"Let's get you inside and clean your cut up. Hopefully you won't need stitches."

***

Mom says the wound isn't deep enough for stitches and that I should be okay. She cleans the cut and dabs anti-bacteria on it so it couldn't be infected.

Dad comes home half an hour later. Avery and I run to him, hugging him tightly.

"Are you kids okay?" he asks us. Both of our parents work several minutes out of Brooke's Creek, and thankfully weren't in the path of the tornado.

"We're okay," I answer.

"I was so scared," Avery sobs.

"You're safe now," Dad answers. "You both are."

"The tornado isn't coming back?"

"No, the tornado isn't coming back."

I pull away from Dad, telling him I was going to go outside and see Jeremy. I step outside, expecting his car to be parked in the driveway or the street, but no cars was there. His parents didn't seem to be home either yet.

I sit on the front step, watching for his car to come down the street at any moment. I don't think he will be too long, unless he is unable to get through the streets that could be blocked by debris. There was still no cell service, so I couldn't call him.

The street felt silent, like everyone had completely

disappeared once the storm ended. Not one single car came down the street, or a person wasn't walking. In the distance I hear sirens as emergency vehicles rushed to rescue people and assist the badly injured.

I kept thinking about Moxie, wondering if the tornado had hit the grocery store. Was she safe there? Or maybe the twister had missed it. I wish I could call her, but who knows when we will get cell service back.

Maybe I can head over to the store while I wait for Jeremy to return.

I head inside, where Mom has decided to make sandwiches for dinner, getting all of the ham and cheese out of the fridge until we get the power back on. Honestly, my appetite wasn't even there.

"Mom, I'm going to see Moxie," I tell her. "I need to know she is okay."

She nods. "I won't stop you. Just be careful out there, okay?"

"I will."

"Have you heard from Jeremy yet?"

I shake my head. "No, he isn't back yet. Neither are his parents."

"I'm sure they will all be back soon. Go and check on Moxie. Make sure you're back before dark."

I grab my bicycle from the garage, and head towards the torn streets. I bite my lip as I passed distressed people who are now completely homeless. It made me feel bad that I still have a house to come home to, and these people don't. I should feel grateful, but it honestly didn't feel right. People dig through the rubble, trying to find some of their belongings, and anyone who might be still trapped underneath. Others walked around, unsure where to go.

I reach to where the grocery store once stood. It's half standing, while the rest of it was completely gone. I let out a cry, hoping Moxie was safe. I see her car in the parking lot with another car that's on top of it. A few people walk around, completely dazed.

"Excuse me," I call out to a middle-aged couple. "Do you know if there's anyone inside of the grocery store still?"

"Everyone got out safely," the woman responds.

I sigh with relief. That means Moxie most likely went home from here. I thank the couple and head to Moxie's house, a few streets away from the store, which I almost struggle to find. When I get there, my heart went out completely to Moxie and her family. Their home was completely destroyed. Nothing was left standing. Their whole street had been flattened.

Moxie is out on what is supposed to be their front lawn, but it's filled with trash. She is with her parents, her younger brother and sister.

"Moxie!" I call out to her.

She turns to me, her eyes lit up with relief when she sees me. "Oh my gosh, Anna!"

I drop my bike and run to Moxie, hugging her.

"Are you okay?" I ask.

She pulls away. "I am."

"Tell me you were safe when the tornado hit. I saw your car at the grocery store parking lot."

"I was safe. I got there ten minutes before the sirens went off. How about you, Anna? Did you get to your brother's school in time?"

I nod. In my mind I can see the large wedge tornado coming towards me. I may have chased many tornadoes, but having one come towards you and you have seconds to save yourself, is the most terrifying thing ever. It's something I don't ever want to think about.

"I got there just as it was near the school."

"Oh my gosh," Moxie gasps as her hand flew to her mouth. "Tell me you got to shelter in time." She points to my cheek. "Is that how you got hurt? You didn't get to shelter in time?"

"I did. I didn't have time to get to the storm shelter, so I hid in the bathroom. And I had something sharp hit my cheek."

Moxie wraps her arms around me. "I'm so glad you're okay."

"Same thing for you."

"Have you heard anything from Jeremy yet?"

I shake my head as I pull away. "No, nothing. The last time I heard from him was when I was two streets away from the school to inform me about the tornado before the sirens began blaring. But I haven't heard anything from him since. There's no cell service, and he hasn't come home yet."

"I'm sure he will soon. He's probably helping someone or he can't get into town. I heard a lot of debris blocked one of the roads into town."

Moxie is right. Soon he will be back at his house, telling me everything about the chase.

"I'm so sorry about your home," I tell her.

"How's your home?"

"It's still standing. The tornado missed both Jeremy's and my home. We just have a few smashed windows from debris."

"You're so lucky. I don't even know what my family and I are going to do."

"Do you have anywhere to go?"

Moxie shrugs. "I'm not sure. We might stay in a motel for

the night and then stay with family tomorrow."

"Why don't your family stay with me tonight? I'm sure my parents won't mind."

Moxie smiles. "I think my parents will like that. Thanks, Anna."

Chapter 6

A couple of hours past, and Jeremy still hasn't returned home. His parents have and are distressed that they haven't heard from him. Even when there were no bars on my phone, I tried to call him anyway, hoping I could still reach him. There's no dial tone. Hopefully by tomorrow we will get our cell services back.

Moxie's family takes my offer, and comes back to my place. I don't know if my parents were unhappy that I didn't consult with them first about Moxie's family staying with us, but they welcome them with open arms, telling them to stay as long as they want until they are able to find a place to go. They are thinking of staying with family up north from Brooke's Creek. Tomorrow they are going to search the rubble to see if there's anything worth saving from the wreckage.

Later that evening Moxie joins me on the front porch, as we keep watch for Jeremy. The town was in complete darkness, and everything was quiet. Not even dogs in the neighborhood were barking tonight. There were also no clouds in the sky, just the stars shining. It was nice because not every day do we get to see so many stars at night. Avery was in the backyard with Moxie's siblings, looking through his telescope. After the terrible events of the day, it was nice to see the three younger kids together, doing something they can enjoy.

I would be in the backyard with them, but it wasn't something I could do without knowing if Jeremy is alright.

"Can I ask you something?" Moxie says.

I force myself to turn away from the street, and turn to my friend. "Yeah."

"What happened today, is that how it is when you and Jeremy go chasing?"

I shake my head. "No. It's far different. For one, you are chasing the tornado and watching it destroy things as you stay out of the way. But when I saw the tornado coming towards me today, it was like the table was turned and the tornado was chasing me. It was the most terrifying thing I ever experience."

"Our parents were listening to the radio and they were saying that it was likely an EF4 or EF5 tornado that hit us. It's not certain yet until the damage is survey."

As soon as the words slip out of Moxie's mouth, it hits me with realisation. If it was an EF4, it was a repeat of the 1971 F4 tornado. I can't imagine what it must be like for the people who have lived through that day, and how they had to go through it a second time.

Who knew that fifty-one years later there would be another tornado to hit our town on the exact same scale as the last one. It was the second EF4 I have ever seen. Last year we saw one during our chase in Texas. Most tornadoes we see were small ones that were rated an EF2 to EF3. The one we chased yesterday was rated an EF3. An EF5 was the rarest and I have never come across it. I don't think I ever want to after experiencing the strength of this possible EF4 twister.

The door opens and Mom joins us.

"Girls, why don't you come on inside." She gives us a warm smile.

"Jeremy hasn't return home yet," I tell her.

Mom looks over next door. It's completely quiet next door, and I can't imagine what Mr. and Mrs. Hayden must be going through to know where their son was. Have they heard from him yet?

She turns to me. "I know, sweetie. But you can't stay out here all night. Jeremy will be home soon." She looks over at Moxie. "Moxie, I set up two sleeping bags in Anna's room. You and your sister will be sleeping in there. Your brother is sleeping with Avery, and your parents are sleeping in the living room."

"Thank you, Mrs. Wade, for both you and your husband to do this," Moxie says.

Mom smiles. "No worries, Moxie. I'm sure your parents will do the same thing for us."

As much as I don't want to go inside, I follow Moxie and mom inside.

Wherever Jeremy is, I hope he is okay.

✶ ✶ ✶

I don't sleep, and I'm sure Moxie and her sister could either. I lay in the darkness. There is an awful feeling in the pit of my stomach. Something is wrong.

My bedroom door is open a jar, where Moxie's sister wanted to sleep with the door open. Olivia slept with a night light, but with the power still out, the only light is from the candles Mom had put in the hallway. With the door opened, I am able to hear someone knocking at the front door. I sit up, praying silently that it is Jeremy coming over to let me know he is alright.

But it isn't Jeremy's voice I hear. It's Mom and Dad and his parents' voices. The sickening feeling in my stomach worsens.

I climb out of bed and stand by my window that looks out onto the street. With the street lights out, I couldn't see if Jeremy's car was parked in the driveway or not. Perhaps he is downstairs with our parents, and doesn't want to come up here to wake me.

I tip-toe across the floor to head downstairs. Moxie sits up. I'm unsure if she was just lying there asleep or she was already awake.

"What is it, Anna?" she whispers. "Is Jeremy home?"

"I'm not sure. His parents are downstairs."

"Well, then he must be here also."

I want to tell her about the awful feeling in the pit of my stomach, but I don't. Perhaps Moxie is right. Jeremy is downstairs with our parents right now.

Moxie follows me out the door. Her sister also wakes up when she hears us, and follows us out. We head to the kitchen, where we find Moxie's parents sitting down at the table. Dad is leaning up against the kitchen island, his hand rubbing over his chin like he couldn't believe whatever news he has just heard. And there is Mr. and Mrs. Hayden, their backs to me as I walked in. Mom is rubbing a hand over Mrs. Hayden's back, her body trembling as she cried.

There is one person missing in the room: Jeremy.

It was like the room turned to ice the moment I walked in. The adults all turns to Moxie, her sister and I, but their eyes were mostly on me. Mr. and Mrs. Hayden's eyes were red and puffy.

There's a lump in my throat. "What is going on?"

No one speaks for a moment.

Dad turns to me. "Why don't you sit down, Anna?"

I listen to Dad and sit down at the end table in between Mr. Hayden and Moxie's mother. Mr. Hayden reaches across the table and squeezes my hand. Mrs. Hayden doesn't look at me.

"Where's Jeremy?" I ask.

"Anna, something happened this afternoon," Mr. Hayden says. "Julie and I have just come from the hospital."

My stomach drops. I can feel everyone's eyes one me, watching me to see how I'm going to react. No. Whatever Mr. Hayden is about to tell me can't be true.

"Chris' car was swept off the road while he and Jeremy were chasing," Mr. Hayden goes on. "Jeremy was in the car with him. Both of them were killed."

I sit there, frozen from Mr. Hayden's words. No. He has gotten this wrong. Jeremy and his uncle can't be dead. "No, be can't be. Jeremy had his own car."

"I spoke with him before the storm hit, and Jeremy told me he was leaving his car at their meeting point in Plainville. From there, they shared a vehicle for the chase."

I look between Mr. Hayden and his wife, who wouldn't

even look at me as her husband spoke. Mom's hand rests on her shoulder as Mrs. Hayden wipes her eyes with a tissue.

No, none of this makes sense. There was no way Jeremy and Chris were killed by the tornado. Chris knew not to get too close to the danger path. He always kept a safe distance when we chased. What made today different?

"How did they get killed?" my voice chokes as I spoke.

Mr. Hayden shakes his head. "We don't know. We are still searching for answers ourselves. All we know is Chris was found still strapped in his seat belt, while Jeremy was found a few metres from the vehicle. Chris' video camera hasn't been recovered, nor has Jeremy's phone."

Mrs. Hayden forces herself to look at me. "He called me to make sure I was in a safe place, that this tornado was going to hit Brooke's Creek head on. While I was on the phone, something happened. I-I don't know what, but Jeremy and Chris began screaming about the tornado getting closer to them and they needed to get out of the way. The phone went dead after that."

I sit there, taking the news in. This is a nightmare. None of this is real. Perhaps I was struck in the head by something while I was in the restroom of Brooke's Creek Elementary, that maybe I'm in a coma or something. But the things I have seen this afternoon, I can see I'm not in a coma or stuck in some kind of nightmare. It's all reality, and it's something I have never expected.

I don't realize I'm crying until Moxie rushes to my side, wrapping her arms around me as she pulls me into a hug. She chokes on her own sobs when she says, "It's okay, Anna."

"I don't understand what happened," I cry. "I don't believe he got too close. He and Chris are always careful not to get too close during chases."

"Maybe the tornado was rain wrapped, or it shifted before they realized the danger they were in."

"During the live news coverage, they showed it was rain wrapped," Mr. Hayden speaks up. "Chris and Jeremy must have not realized how close they were to it."

Moxie pulls away from me. I cover my face with my hands, sobbing hard. I recall my last phone call with Jeremy just hours ago as the tornado headed towards our town. Was he killed shortly after he had gotten off the phone with me to call his mother?

Someone is talking, but I can't hear them speak.

Hurry, Anna! I recall Jeremy's very last words to me. *I'm over in Plainville. A tornado is on the ground, nearing the freeway into town. You have maybe ten minutes before it hits Brooke's Creek. It's big. It's a wedge tornado! It's violent, and oh gosh, Anna, from the damage I'm seeing, it could be an EF4 or EF5.*

Who knew that was the last thing I would ever hear Jeremy say to me.

Did he know he was in trouble? Did he know he was going to die?

"Anna, sweetie," Dad says, standing beside me and place his hand on my shoulder.

I wipe my eyes and look up at him. When I do, I burst into tears again. He pulls me close to him into a hug.

"Jeremy's gone," I mumble. "He's gone."

"I'm sorry, sweetheart."

Dad stands there for a moment to let me sob into his chest, before he helps me off the chair and cradles me into his arms. Leaving the kitchen, he walks me upstairs to my room.

Chapter 7

I don't remember falling asleep. But when I wake up the next morning, I'm lying on my side, staring out the window. I'm completely paralysed, even when Moxie wakes up, opening the curtains to let the sunlight into the room, I don't move to greet her good morning. She even tells me to get up, but I can't move. Not even to talk. Even when Mom comes into my room to check on me, I can't get up. I don't see the point to.

All I can think about is Jeremy. I replay our last conversation on the phone right before the tornado struck, our time in school, and our last storm chase together. What went wrong yesterday afternoon? Did he know he was too close to the tornado when it became rain wrapped? He knows the danger of getting too close, especially when it becomes rain wrapped. Chris has always been the driver, and knows the danger as well. So why did they get close this time? Or were they in a safe distance but the tornado suddenly shifted its track, putting them in the path of danger, not giving them enough time to get out of the way?

Whatever happened, I will never get to know the answers.

My best friend in the whole world is dead, and I don't know how to live without him.

Before I knew it, two days have passed. Moxie and her family were moving out to stay with family. She promised me she will contact me the moment she is settle in at her temporary place, and wanted me to let her know about Jeremy's funeral.

I force myself out of bed on the day she leaves, farewelling her as her aunt parks her mini-van in front of our house. I hug Moxie tightly, and I told her I was thankful for her being here, even if the past two days I was paralysed in my bed, barely acknowledging her. She understood how I felt, and we cry for the friend who made up our trio.

"When we find a temporary home, I will invite you over," Moxie says. "If you want, we can do something in memory of Jeremy."

I liked that, and knew Jeremy would appreciate it.

Long after Moxie and her family left, I'm still standing on the lawn, watching the Hayden's house, like if maybe I stare at it hard enough, Jeremy would appear. But he doesn't. He's gone. He's never coming back.

A hand touches my shoulder, and I turn to see Mom. She gives me a small smile.

"Why don't you come inside, sweetie?" she says. "We can talk if you like. I'm about to make lunch soon."

I didn't want to talk. At least not straight away. I wanted to be alone. And as for food, I haven't eaten for two days, not since I found out about Jeremy. Even when I forced myself out of bed this morning to say goodbye to Moxie, I still didn't quite have the appetite.

I know my parents mean well, and they want me to open up to what I feel deep inside about what happened to Jeremy, but I don't know if opening up to them is something I can do right now. I have been lying in bed for two days, and I had to do everything I could to force myself out of bed this morning. School was cancelled for the rest of the week, maybe for the rest of the term until our town can get back on our feet. There was no word on when we were going to have our graduation or if we were even going to have a prom this year. With no school in session, I have no idea when I was seeing Moxie again. If I go back inside, I will only lock myself away in my room.

What I need is to get away from the house for a bit.

I give my mom a small smile. "Thanks, Mom, but I'm not hungry."

Mom looks at me with concern. "Honey, you haven't eaten for two days. Come in and eat some lunch."

"Maybe later, Mom. Right now, I just need to be alone. Do you mind if I take my bike and go out for a while?"

Mom returns a small smile. "Of course you can, sweetie. Don't go too far, and be careful of debris." The debris most likely would not be all cleared up for months.

I promised I wouldn't. I grab my bike from the garage, and set off down the street, unclear where I was going. Riding down the street was painful passing the debris. Searching for anyone who may be trapped under the rubble has stopped, but there were people around still trying to search for their belongings. It was confirmed yesterday that it was indeed an EF4 tornado that struck our town. Once the rubble gets cleared up, it was going to be weird seeing everything empty in this town. Is this how it felt when the tornado hit the town in 1971?

I find myself by the gas station Jeremy and I had gone to when we were ten, where we had seen our very first funnel cloud in the corn fields. The tornado had missed both the gas station and corn fields.

I stand by the gas station with my bike picturing Jeremy and I at ten years old, sheltering from the hail that had fallen. I will never forget that day when Jeremy was so enthusiastic about seeing his very first tornado. Who knew that eight years later, one would have taken his life. The one thing that he was passionate about is what killed him.

Tornadoes are incredible and an amazing piece of nature. It's alright when they are out in the open, away from anything they can destroy, but when they head towards towns and metropolitan areas, that's when they become deadly.

Staring out at the corn field, I think about the movie *Twister*. I remember when the movie ended after we watched it for the first time, Jeremy says, "I'm going to be just like Bill Harding when I grow up."

I laugh. "You can't be Bill Harding. He is fictional."

"Yes, but I'm going to chase tornadoes one day."

"Why? Tornadoes are scary."

"I think they are fascinating. I want to do what Bill and Jo do, chase tornadoes and get up close to study them."

Bill Paxton may have played a fictional storm chaser, but Jeremy was really inspired by his character to become a meteorologist someday. The movie drew him to something so deadly, but yet at the same time it was thrilling. Jeremy studied tornadoes, and wanted to learn every single thing about them. He wanted to someday take part in research to improve lead time, which was currently thirteen minutes, and just knowing how the storm system really works. With the help of social media, a tornado warning can be issue in advance with a bigger chance of preparing for safety. Maybe the more studies and data collected, we could improve so much more in the lead time. Or maybe we will discover something we don't already know about tornadoes.

What was going through Jeremy's mind when he was caught in the winds that quite possibly blown him and Chris off the road?

I sit down on the side of the road, my bike lying on the ground beside me, my eyes never leaving the corn field as I thought back to the memory when we were ten. I will never know what happened that afternoon when he was killed. His parents have searched for Chris' video camera, but hadn't been able to find it. Maybe it's a good thing they haven't found it because the footage of what happened during the chase will break me. Besides, it most likely would be smashed, and no one will ever be able to see the footage.

I pull out my phone and pull up the last photo of Jeremy and I. It doesn't make sense to me to what happen, how he was always careful, and that day he wasn't. But now all I have is memories.

I stay on the side of the road before I force myself to get back on my bike, and head home. The last thing I wanted was for my parents to worry, and come looking for me.

* * *

Later that evening was a thunderstorm. There was no tornado warning, thank goodness. Just a normal storm. I sit at my window, watching the lightning and rain pour down. I could imagine Jeremy calling me about now, discussing with me about the storm. I even look at my phone, like he was going to call me at any second. But the phone remains silent. All there is a text message from Moxie in which I haven't reply to yet. I should really do so.

I open up her message.

Hey, just letting you know I made it to my grandparents. I will chat with you tomorrow.

I didn't have the energy to respond, so I send a thumbs up emoji instead.

A knock comes from my door. When I look over, it opens before I allow the person to enter. Avery stands there with his hand on the handle.

His lips tremble. "Anna, I'm scared."

I wave him over. "Come here."

He hurries over to me as lightning flashes, lighting up the room. He makes it to the window seat and sits in my lap just as the thunder rumbles loudly.

"Don't be scared," I tell my brother. "It's just a storm."

"What if the tornado returns?"

I wasn't sure how to answer my brother's question because who knows when the next tornado will come through this town.

"I can't tell you when the next tornado will strike, but I can guarantee we won't get another one tonight."

"That day was the scariest thing I have ever gone through. I don't ever want to go through it again."

I gently rock my brother, hoping it will comfort him. "Same here, Avery."

We sit there in silence for a moment, watching the storm.

Whenever the thunder rumbles, Avery flinches.

"I'm sorry about Jeremy," Avery tells me.

"Thanks, Avery."

"What we went through the other day, is that how it is when you storm chase?"

I shake my head. "No. It's completely different. You are staying out of the tornado's path. But storm chasing can be thrilling and scary all at the same time because tornadoes are unpredictable."

"Do you think you will storm chase again?"

I'm quiet for a moment, unsure how to answer. It was a question I wasn't expecting my brother to ask me. It wasn't even a question I have asked myself yet. I doubt I will be going storm chasing this June like Jeremy had planned with his cousins. Without Jeremy, I don't know if I will ever storm chase again.

"I don't know," I answer as I glance out the window, a lightning bolt lights up the sky. "Maybe."

Chapter 8

The first week was hard to get through. I was thankful I didn't have to go to school. There was no way I could deal with going there and not seeing Jeremy in the halls. Our gym was currently in used for people who had nowhere to go, and our mayor was organizing a memorial for the twenty people who lost their lives in the tornado. School was cancelled for the rest of the term, and so is prom. There's still no word on the graduation, but I think the principal is trying to decide where it should be held.

I talked to Moxie a few times, where she helped me to get through the week. Instead of focusing on his death, we talked about the memories. Moxie found ways to put a smile on my face. I also finally sat down to talk to Mom, telling her how I felt, and she listened carefully. Talking about Jeremy and everything that happened with the tornado helped, like a weight lifted off my shoulders. I saw Jeremy's parents a few times. They weren't coping well, and look as they haven't had a wink of sleep. I feel sorry for Mrs. Hayden the most. She not only lost her son, but her brother. Mom and Dad helped them with chores, and we had them over for dinner a few nights.

They break the news to us that they plan to sell their house in a few months once things go back to normal here. They can't bear to live here knowing Jeremy is gone. I couldn't imagine the Haydens not living next door. I grew up with them. If Jeremy is gone and his parents plan to move, how will my life be without them?

The funeral for Chris and Jeremy was two weeks later after the tragic incident. In some way it all still felt like some kind of nightmare, like this wasn't real life. Even as I walk into the church and see the photographs of Jeremy and Chris, smiling at us, next to the caskets, I didn't want to accept this is reality. I didn't want to accept that my best friend in the entire world was gone, and I will never storm chase with him again.

But I had to accept it, even if I don't want to.

Moxie sits with me and my family at the funeral. We sit in the third row, while the Haydens and family sat in the front and second row. Moxie holds my hand the whole time as the funeral conductor talks about Chris and Jeremy's lives.

The whole time the funeral conductor speaks, I stare at the photo of Jeremy, his smiling face staring at everyone in the audience. It was a photo of him that was taken recently. It was the beginning of March, which meant the beginning of tornado season. Jeremy was preparing to go south-east to Dixie Alley for the weekend with Chris, and Mrs. Hayden had snapped the photo of him, blue skies and fluffy white clouds in the distance. He was excited that day to be able to go storm chasing after having to wait for nine months for the next season.

After the ceremony ends, people stand around chatting. Mr. and Mrs. Hayden hug Moxie and me, thanking us for being his friend. My parents talked to them while my brother chatted to one of Jeremy's cousins who is the same age as him.

I stay close to Moxie, not wanting to talk to anyone besides her.

"Hey, do you want to go get some ice cream?" Moxie asks me. We were invited to the wake, but I was really not in the mood to attend it. I don't think I can step foot in the Haydens' home without Jeremy being there.

"Sure," I answer.

Moxie was spending the night with me before she goes back to her family tomorrow.

"Anna?"

I turn to see a guy with dark hair who had called my name. He was fairly young, maybe a couple of years older than me. Besides him is a woman who was slightly shorter than him with blonde hair. I instantly recognized them from their parents' wedding when I was invited to it.

I smile at the both of them. "Hello, Jonah, Lindy. It's good to see you again."

Jonah returns the smile. "It's good to see you. So has Jeremy talked to you about our plans for the summer?"

I nod. "He has. He told me about it the day before he died."

"He mentioned you were a photographer," Lindy says.

"I am. I often come on chases to photograph the weather."

"Listen, Anna, I know your plans may have changed this summer with what happened with Jeremy, but Lindy and I are still wondering if you would like to come along with us?"

I stare at him, completely unsure what I wanted. I wasn't even sure if I wanted to storm chase anymore. Not without my best friend and his passion for storms. It just wouldn't be the same without him.

"I don't know if I want to go storm chasing anymore," I admit.

Jonah nods. "I completely understand, Anna. But if you ever change your mind, you're welcome to tag along." He reaches inside his suit jacket and pulls out his wallet. He pulls out a business card and hands it to me. "If you ever change your mind and would like to chase, give me a call."

I take the card, glimpsing at it where it had his picture over a background of dark storm clouds with his name and contact information. "Thank you."

"We were really looking forward to having you both with us next month," Lindy says. "Jonah and I haven't storm chase with Jeremy or Uncle Chris for a while, and we thought it would be awesome to do one with them before tornado season is over. We even wanted to share with Jeremy with what we have been learning in our first year of college. If you're still able to come along with us, it would be awesome to have you. We will be going on break soon before our exams start, and we thought of doing a chase in honor of Jeremy and Chris. We would love for you to join us."

I thank them both again for the invitation. Saying goodbye, Jonah and Lindy walk away and heads to talk to someone else.

"Do you think you will go storm chasing with Jeremy's cousins?" Moxie asks me.

I shrug. A million things were running through my head right now, and I don't think I'm in the right headspace to decide on anything. "I don't know."

"How come I have never met any of his cousins before?"

"I don't know. Maybe because they live in Kansas and don't visit here often."

"Anna, are you really going to waste this opportunity to storm chase with these meteorology students? I mean, I know you aren't going to study meteorology like Jeremy, but maybe you could learn something with them that you didn't get to with Chris and Jeremy. Plus, they are doing this in honor of them."

I turn to Moxie. She's right. Why would I want waste this opportunity? I mean, Jeremy *wanted* me to have this opportunity with him and his cousins. I could imagine the photos I could take if I were to get up close to tornadoes, ones that I have never had the opportunity with Chris and Jeremy. But still, could I even do this without him? Even if his cousins decides that the chase is in honor of them? "I don't know if I want to keep chasing."

"Even when Jeremy's uncle organized this for you all to chase together?"

"It's not like it matters anymore."

"I'm sure he wouldn't want you to give it up."

Does it matter if I gave up storm chasing? It has always been Jeremy's hobby, in which he dragged me along to do. He was the weather enthusiast, not me. I got into photography while on one. If he isn't here anymore, what use does storm chasing have for me? Besides, I don't think I want to see another tornado as long as I live.

"It was something Jeremy and I did together," I explain. "I probably wouldn't even do it if it wasn't for him."

Moxie stares at me, looking like she wants to say more but

chooses not to get into an argument right here.

I look over at Jonah and Lindy. Lindy is talking to someone, and Jonah chooses the exact moment to look my way. As soon as he does, my heart jumps at the sight of him. We lock eyes with each other briefly before he turns away.

"You should definitely take the opportunity to go storm chasing with Jeremy's cousins. Chris organized it so Jeremy could learn from his cousins who are studying, and you had the opportunity to pursue your photography. Besides, you said you want to work on your photography over the summer to build up a portfolio for internships. And school is out right now for the rest of the year. We are just waiting to hear about graduation. So why not pursue this opportunity? It's a chase honoring them."

I think about her words for a second, remembering what Jeremy wanted me to do. But still, how can I go storm chasing without my best friend?

"I don't know," I answer.

"You never know what could happen when you do. Just think about it, Anna. Think about what Jeremy would want for you to do. If I was into storms as much as you two, I would gladly go on a chase with you. But chasing storms don't interest me, no matter how thrilling it sounds. If you don't want to do it, fine. I completely understand. At least do it for Jeremy in his honor."

Moxie has a point, but it felt all so soon to be making this decision. Yeah, Jeremy most likely wouldn't want me to stop chasing, but I couldn't do it without him. For a few nights I have had nightmares about the tornado. I always see it coming towards me, and there's nowhere to run. There was one dream where Jeremy was running towards me, telling me to take shelter. I try reaching for him, but when I do, the tornado sweeps him up. How can I chase knowing this deadly storm took away my best friend?

* * *

I keep thinking about what Moxie had said to me earlier. We don't talk about it for the rest of the afternoon. I think about what she said, along with what Jeremy had said when he had told me about the plans for the summer.

This June was supposed to be ours. We were going to spend it chasing storms. He had said it was the perfect opportunity to build up my portfolio. I just don't know how I could do it without him.

When Moxie falls asleep, I open my laptop and scroll through the pictures I had taken on our previous chases. There's a few of me and Jeremy with a tornado in the distance. There's a couple I had snapped of Jeremy with his back to me, as he faces the twisters in the distance or he is studying the formation of the clouds. I also taken photos of the landscape of the Midwest, and many of dark blue-greenish clouds, a couple of lightning strikes and there are ones with tornadoes.

Anna, think of all the amazing photos you can take this summer to build up the portfolio you want for internships and job interviews. Not only storms, but we will be out on the road, and you can take amazing pictures of the landscape or whatever pictures you want to take, Jeremy's words echo in my head.

He not only wanted me to build up my portfolio, but he also wanted me to sell my photographs. It's not something I wanted, but maybe I could consider it. One of my goals is to have my own photography business and sell my prints. I don't know if I will sell any of them to magazines. It's probably something I won't decide until I go to college.

On my desk beside my laptop is a photograph of Jeremy and I, standing next to the car his parents had gotten for his sixteenth birthday. I stare at it.

Seventeen. He would have turned eighteen next month. My birthday followed shortly after his in July. How could Jeremy's life be cut so short? It wasn't right.

"Why does storm chasing mean so much to you, Jeremy? I whisper aloud at his photograph. "How can I go on a chase with your cousins without you? I can't storm chase without you. It won't be the same."

The tears start to fall, and I quickly wipe them. Jeremy isn't going to want me to cry over him. He will want me to be happy.

And I'm happy most when I take photos.

I get off the chair and sit by the window. The sky is clear tonight. Would I be crazy to turn this opportunity down to chase with meteorology students? Chris was an amateur storm chaser. When he first learned what Jeremy wanted to do, he started driving Jeremy across the Mid-west to watch storms. He sometimes chased with him, and then another time he would go on one with Jonah. Jeremy was so thrilled his uncle had invited his cousins along, as he hasn't chased much with them, maybe a few times when he had visited Jonah and storm watched with Jonah's father, who is a storm spotter. But never did Chris chased with his nephews at the same time. Going out on the road with his cousins was Jeremy's chance to see what they had learned in their meteorology degree, and learn from them before he started classes at the end of August.

Like Moxie had said, Jeremy would have wanted me to keep chasing.

Chapter 9

When Jeremy and I were younger and had trouble sleeping, we would put on our favorite movie in hope when it's over it will help us fall asleep. But I didn't watch my favorite. Not tonight. I watch Jeremy's favorite instead: *Twister*.

I sneak out of my room without waking Moxie, and head downstairs to stick our copy of the movie in the DVD player. I snuggle the couch cushion against my chest as I watch it in the dark room at a volume that I could hear and not disturb anyone else. As I watch the movie, I picture myself as Jo and Jeremy as Bill. I try to understand how this movie drew his fascination towards tornadoes and his dream to be a meteorologist, storm chasing in between his career.

Despite the destructive damage they can caused, tornadoes are the most fascinating thing I find in the weather system.

How this rotating column of air forms and moves. It's also something that's very hard to study as getting close to it is difficult and dangerous. There's so many things to learn about these storms that we don't already know about. Jeremy hoped to take part in research once he gets into college, anything that will help understand tornadoes better.

Meteorology wasn't my thing, but photography was for me. I'm not sure how in a way it could help with studying tornadoes. I guess taking pictures of the damage path could help identifying the strength of the twister, but I wasn't interested in photographing that. I wanted to capture the clouds and the formation of it. Capturing the weather is what I wanted. Avery loved my photos I take of thunderstorms with lightning strikes, especially the ones I have taken at night. They were my favorite photographs too, the way the lightning brightens up the night sky. But now I wasn't even sure if he liked the idea of thunderstorms, or if he was just still in shock from the twister.

When the movie ends, I sit there for a moment as I watch the credits roll. I hug the cushion tightly and cry. The whole movie makes me think about Jeremy, and I still didn't know how I could storm chase without him. But the idea of studying them to help save people lives from tornadoes was his passion. The weather fascinated him. Getting close to a tornado, feeling the wind and having that adrenaline rush is what he craved for. I imagine him working for the National Weather Service someday, forecasting the weather and warning people to get to safety.

"Anna?"

I turn to see Moxie walking into the living room. She glances at the TV where the credits had finish rolling, and it was now at the title menu. She turns back to me and joins me on the couch. Moving the pillow from me, she hugs me tightly.

"I miss him," I cry into her shoulder.

"I miss him, too, Anna."

"Why did this happen?"

"I don't know, Anna. It's just one of those things you can't control."

We sit there in the dark, sobbing together.

"Anna, I need you do something for me," Moxie says as she pulls away, wiping her eyes. "I know you feel lost, but you need to do this for me. Not just for me, but for Jeremy. He would want you to do this. I can't stand to see you fall to pieces. Maybe you and Jeremy storm chase for two different reasons, but I can't let you be lost. Go out and chase tornadoes with his cousins. Go out there and make Jeremy proud."

I wipe my eyes and nod. Moxie is right. I need to do this. I need to take Jeremy's cousins' offer of chasing with them. "Okay. I will do it."

* * *

When the morning comes, I leave Moxie to sleep and crept downstairs. After I calm down last night, we had gone back to bed and I managed to get some sleep. I headed to the kitchen where my parents are, getting ready for work. With school out, I was home taking care of my brother. He's been enjoying sleeping in.

Dad is sipping a cup of coffee while Mom is making breakfast for the both of them.

"Mom, Dad, can I talk to you?" I ask them.

They look over at me with a small smile.

"Of course, Anna," Dad says.

I join my parents at the kitchen island.

"I know right now that storm chasing is something you probably wouldn't want me to do," I say. "But I'm thinking of going. I was chatting with two of Jeremy's cousins at the funeral. They are currently in their first year of college, studying meteorology. The day before the tornado hit, Jeremy and I skipped school and went chasing. He told me that his uncle had organize teaming up with his cousins for a chase in June. I'm not sure if I'm going to go next month, but his cousins have organized a chase in honor of Chris and Jeremy. I want to go with them."

Dad holds up his hand, signalling me not to say anything more. "You went chasing the day before the tornado hit?"

I give a guilty look between my parents. Maybe I shouldn't have let that slip out of my mouth. "Yes. We skipped school, and went on one without Chris."

Dad frowns. "Anna, you know the both of you aren't allow to go without Jeremy's uncle being present. What if…" He pauses for a second and I know what he is immediately thinking about. "What if what happened to Jeremy and his uncle happened to you too?"

"I know the dangers, Dad. Jeremy did too. What happened to him and his uncle was a freak accident. And I'm sorry I went off without telling you guys."

"If you ever do plan to go chasing again, Anna, do make sure you aren't doing it alone," Mom says. "Your father and I don't want anything to happen to you."

I nod. "I promise. So, about Jeremy's cousins. Is it possible I can go chasing with them?"

My parents look at each other before turning to me.

"Maybe," Dad says. "We haven't met Jeremy's cousins before, even if you have met them at the funeral. We don't want you to go off with someone your mother and I don't know."

I nod. "Of course. I can organize for Jonah and Lindy to come over here so you guys can meet."

"That will be great, sweetie." Dad glances at his watch. "I need to get going."

He finishes the rest of his coffee before kissing Mom goodbye. He turns to me, kissing my forehead. Before he leaves, he points a finger at me, giving me a serious look.

"We will discuss about you going chasing alone with Jeremy later," Dad tells me. "For now, you have a good day, okay?"

"Have a good day, Dad."

Dad leaves the kitchen and is soon out the front door.

"Are you sure storm chasing is something you want to do, Anna?" Mom asks me once we are alone, her face full of concern.

I nod. "I'm sure, Mom. At first, I thought what's the point of chasing without Jeremy, but Moxie convinced me not to stop chasing just because he is gone. She encouraged me to go on a chase and take pictures like I always do. Plus, Jeremy wanted me to take photos for my portfolio."

Mom smiles. "That's good, sweetie. I'm glad Moxie convinced you to go. I know it's going to be hard without Jeremy, but Moxie is right. He wouldn't want you to stop."

"He wouldn't," Moxie says as she strolls into the kitchen. She stands beside me. "How are you feeling, Anna?"

I smile at her. "I'm feeling much better. All thanks to you."

Moxie returns a smile. "That's good to hear."

Mom quickly finishes making her breakfast. "Anna, your

father and I will talk more about the storm chasing later. See if you can contact Jeremy's cousins, and arrange for them to come over."

I smile at Mom. "I will."

I couldn't wait for my parents to meet Jonah and Lindy. I'm glad Moxie talked me into continuing with chasing. I can imagine Jeremy smiling at me, enthusiastic telling me what to look forward to on the chase.

If my parents allow me to go on this chase, I'm going to make Jeremy proud.

Chapter 10

I take a look around my room one last time, making sure I had everything in my duffel bag. With school out and my graduation has been organized to be at the beginning of June, we figured it was the perfect time to do a chase in honor of Chris and Jeremy. Jonah and Lindy came over the day after I told my parents about them, and they chatted about what I will be doing. Jonah and Lindy promised my parents that I will be safe at all times, and they won't let anything happen to me like what happened with Jeremy and Chris.

My eyes land on the photograph I had of Jeremy and me on my desk, one that I took when Chris took us on our first chase together. I walk over to it and pick it up.

"I'm going on a chase with your cousins," I say to the photograph. "It won't be the same without you, but I promise I will make you proud while I'm out there."

"Anna?"

I turn around to see my brother standing at the door. I put the photograph down on my desk.

"What's up, buddy?" I ask him.

"Why are you going on a storm chase after everything that has happened?"

I walk over to my brother. "Everything will be alright, Avery. It's just something I need to do."

"But why? Aren't you scared? What if what happened to Jeremy happens to you?"

I kneel down at my brother's height, and place my hands on his shoulders. Avery bites his lip like if he doesn't do it, he might burst into tears.

"Avery, listen to me. I'm scared every time I go out there to chase because I have no idea what's going to happen. I do it because there's something thrilling and terrifying about it. What happened with Jeremy and his uncle was an accident. I'm going to come home. I promise you that, Avery."

Avery nods, but doesn't look convince of my promise.

"Remember, I come home every time when I used to go on chases with Jeremy. Hey, I will tell you what. How about I give you a call every day to let you know I'm safe? Will that make you feel better?"

Avery nods with a smile. "It would, Anna."

I return the smile. "Okay. I will call you every day."

My brother hugs me tightly. "I love you, Anna."

"I love you too, Avery."

Dad comes up behind my brother. "Anna?"

I glance up at him. "Yeah?"

"Jonah and Lindy are here. Are you all set?"

I pull away from Avery and stand up, nodding. "Yes, I'm all set."

Dad smiles. "Okay, well I will meet you downstairs." He puts a hand around Avery's shoulders and steer him away from my door. "Come on, Avery. Let's wait downstairs for your sister."

Dad steers my brother out of the room. Taking one more look around my room, telling myself that this chase is all for Jeremy, I grab my bag from my bed and head downstairs.

* * *

My favorite thing about chasing is driving out to the middle of nowhere. There may not be anything there, but I always enjoy the scenery, and how peaceful it is out here.

Once we leave my place, Jonah at the wheel heads out west towards Texas. There's a storm system building up near the Texas panhandle. But first before we head out there, Jonah drives to a gas station just outside of Brooke's Creek, where he was picking up two members of his team who were meeting him there.

He pulls into a gas station where two guys were waiting out front. Jonah pulls up near them.

"Hey, guys," Jonah greets them, unbuckling his seat belt. "Did you get out here okay?"

Jonah, Lindy and I get out of the car.

"Yeah, we got out here without any trouble," the guy with a gold chain around his neck with the letter S attached to it says.

"I'm going to go and get some coffee for the road," Lindy announces. "Anyone want one?"

We all declined Lindy's offer, and she headed inside the gas station. Once she is gone, Jonah gestures me to the guys. Up close I could see they were brothers, fraternal twins perhaps. They looked so alike with crystal blue eyes, dark hair and a square jaw. They both wear a black t-shirt with a twister printed on it. The other guy wears a similar necklace to the other guy, but with an O.

"Guys, I would like you to meet Anna. She is joining us on the chase this week. Anna, these are my good friends Owen and Sawyer."

"It's nice to meet you, Anna," the guy with the letter S necklace points to himself. "I'm Sawyer." He points to Owen. "And this is my brother, Owen."

"It's nice to meet you both," I say.

"Same thing for you," Owen answers. "It's great to have you on the chase."

"Have you guys gotten food yet?" Jonah asks them.

Sawyer shakes his head. "No. We thought we would wait for you guys before we brought anything."

"Okay, well you guys go in and grab food. I'm going to fill up the car before we get out on the road."

The twins head on inside.

Jonah turns to me. "Go on inside and grab some food before we head off. We won't be stopping anywhere once we finish here."

I nod, and head on inside the store. I wasn't sure what I wanted to eat, or what we were going to do for breakfast tomorrow. So I grab a box of Pop Tarts. For lunch I grab a BLT club sandwich, along with a bag of nuts and chocolates for snacks. Wandering the store makes me think of Jeremy for a second to how we loved grabbing anything to take on the road with us whenever we chase.

Once we got everything we need, we gather around outside as a group. Jonah and Lindy studied the radar, deciding where in the Texas Panhandle a tornado is more likely to form from the supercell that is building up. Sawyer and Owen peek over their shoulders at the radar, and gave suggestions also.

As Jonah talks, discussing with everyone in the team if they agree with the location that we were heading to, I imagine Jeremy amongst this team. He would be getting excited and wanting to get on the road already instead of standing around and discussing where to go. I try not to think about him too much, because the last thing I wanted was to be sad. I wanted to be out on this chase and make Jeremy proud. He wouldn't want me to be mourning over him and stop doing what the two of us loved doing together.

Back in the car, we head west towards Texas. Owen is riding in the front seat with Lindy at the wheel. Jonah sits beside me and Sawyer is on the other side sitting behind his brother.

"Anna, have you ever intercepted a tornado before?" Lindy asks me.

I shake my head. "No, never. When I chased with Chris and Jeremy, we never did any of that stuff."

"Well, I promise you on this chase it will be different to your other ones. One of our goals today is to try and get a probe in the path of a tornado. Will that be something you're comfortable with?"

I let the question hang in the air for a bit, unsure how I should answer. Jeremy and Chris never studied the science side to tornadoes, so we have never used probes before. Chris did chases as a hobby for his nephew to live his dream of being a storm chaser. Jeremy, on the other hand, wanted to study the science side, but was waiting to get his meteorology degree to do that. In the meantime, he chased tornadoes for fun, to get experience and what to expect once he started college. From the distance he studied the clouds and the vortex, watching how it forms and moves. When he wasn't chasing, he researched everything there is to know about mesocyclones and the supercells that produce them. Jeremy would definitely have made an excellent meteorologist.

Me, I wasn't into science. I hated it in school. Studying the science side of tornadoes was different for me, as I have always view them from the distance with my camera. Helping Jonah and his team will be like living Jeremy's dream.

"I should be okay with it," I answer.

"Let me know if there's anything you aren't comfortable doing."

I promise I will. I may not have been on a chase for two weeks, and I still get the chills whenever I think about being inside the tornado. But I know I'm capable of doing this.

* * *

Towards the north west the clouds were building up once we reach the Texas/Oklahoma boarder.

Turning off the interstate, we stop to fill up. Jonah takes a moment to survey the clouds. We weren't far from our destination to where we were sure the storm will produce a tornado.

I haven't been to the Texas Panhandle before. Looking around at the landscape, it was mostly dry land. I enjoy chasing out in these parts of Tornado Alley, away from the towns and busy areas. But of course, a tornado's path is always unpredictable, and they don't always miss the towns.

I take my camera and snap a few photos of the landscape with the clouds in the distance.

We don't stop at the gas station for long, getting back in the vehicle, we continue heading northwest.

In a small town call Darcy, the clouds are darker. We drive a few minutes outside of the town to the south of the storm. Pulling over, we get out to study the clouds. Thunder rumbles across the plains, and I manage to snap a photo of a lightning bolt striking the ground.

Jonah stands near me, watching me. Above us the clouds move quickly.

"There's a lot of rotation over there," Owen points to a spot near us in the field.

We don't observe the storm for long as we had to quickly escape inside the vehicle as the hail comes down. Jonah is at the wheel now. Owen manages to grab a hail stone before hopping into the car.

"Look at the size of this hailstone!" Owen says, holding the baseball size hailstone up at us. "It's massive!"

We sit there, watching the hail hammer down on us. One stone manages to hit the windshield and cracks it.

"Hey," Lindy points at something in the distance. "Northwest from here I think I can see something that looks like a wall cloud."

We turn in our seats to get a look at what Lindy has spotted. It was hard to spot with the rain that is now coming down heavy, but I could just spot it in the distance.

"Let's make our way towards northwest to get a better look at it," Jonah suggests.

Doing a U-turn across the road, we head in the direction

of where Lindy had spotted the wall cloud. There's a couple of other storm chasers parked on the side of the road, observing the storm. The rain gives us poor visibility, even with the windshield wipers moving fast. With the crack in the windshield from the hailstone it was blocking Jonah's view of the road. Winding down the window, he pokes his head out.

"I hope this rain stops so we can get a good view of the funnel when it drops," Jonah says. "How's the radar looking, Owen? Any hook echoes?"

Owen glances at his phone where he has the radar displayed. I can't read the radar map, and never know what I'm looking for on it, even when Jeremy explains it to me. "I can see a hook echo. Let's keep moving towards the wall cloud and see if a funnel will form."

"I get a feeling if a tornado does form, it's going to be rain wrapped," Jonah says. "Let me know if you get any visual on the funnel."

Everyone's phone goes off at the same time. I pick up mine to see that a tornado warning has been issued for our area.

"Jonah, a tornado warning has been issue," Sawyer says.

The warning is then issued on the radio.

"Okay, everyone. A warning has been issued. Keep a look out for a funnel or any debris. There's a chance it could also be rain wrapped, so keep your eyes appeal."

We keep driving, the rain belting down hard. Hopefully we can see through this rain soon.

I stare out of the window on my right where the wall cloud was, that we could no longer see because of the rain. But I squint my eyes at something that I can just make out in the distance.

"I think I see a funnel," I point out.

Jonah isn't able to really see as he keeps his eyes on the road. The others glance out to follow my gaze to where I think I may have seen the funnel cloud.

"I can't locate anything," Lindy says. "It's hard to see anything in this rain."

Jonah pulls over to get a glimpse of the tornado. Now that he has stopped the vehicle, he is able to get a better look of the rain wrapped tornado. It's a white funnel that appears to be a stove pipe. It's just barely visible in the rain.

"Alright, let's see if we can find a road that heads towards the tornado," Jonah says. He turns to Owen. "Are you able to see any roads turning right up here?"

Owen pulls up the GPS. "There are roads, Jonah, but they aren't paved."

Jonah curses, hitting the steering wheel. With all of the rain we have, there is no way we can drive onto the muddy dirt roads. Especially if we were to get stuck and not able to see the rain wrapped tornado.

He sits there for a moment, unsure what to do.

"Okay," he finally says. "Let's keep driving, see if we can get ahead."

Jonah pulls back onto the road and we follow the direction of the tornado, in hope the rain slows down a bit so we were able to get a better glimpse of it.

Chapter 11

The tornado dissipates before we get a chance to get close to it.

Ending the chase for the day, we drive to a motel for the night. We weren't able to get to the damage path, and it looked like it didn't hit any towns. Not sure if there was any damage to rural properties, but I hope there wasn't.

Booking two different rooms, I room with Lindy. I offer to help her pay, but she tells me she has it covered. Once we drop our belongings in the room, we headed out to a small diner in town for dinner.

"So, Anna, how did you find today?" Jonah asks me.

I chew my burger before answering, nodding. "I enjoy it even though we didn't get to see the tornado very well."

"Well, hopefully tomorrow we have a better chance of seeing one," Sawyer says. "The forecast shows a lot of storm activity around Oklahoma and Kansas. We will check the forecast again tomorrow morning, and decide on which storm to chase."

"How did you get into storm chasing, Anna?" Lindy wants to know. "Have you always been fascinated by the weather like Jeremy was?"

Of course, this question was bound to come up eventually. I have been enjoying today that it never occurred to me. At the back of my mind, yes, Jeremy was there as I thought about him and how he would act on this chase. Mostly I thought about him when we were out on the road. But as soon as the excitement of the storm develop, he slipped my mind for a brief moment. I wanted to enjoy the moment instead of thinking about him that could easily give me second thoughts or getting out there and chasing storms without him.

But if I'm going to chase with these people, I needed to be open and not feel like I would break down at any memory of my best friend. It was important to stay alert when storm chasing. Jeremy wouldn't want me to break down because of a memory I had of us storm chasing. I needed to remember that I wasn't the only one here coping with a loss. Lindy and Jonah had lost him too, and were trying not to let their loss interfere with their chase. They needed to be focus so we are all safe on the road.

"Jeremy had always been fascinated by storms," I explain. "But it wasn't until we watched *Twister* when we were ten, that he became completed hooked on storms. He started chasing thunderstorms around our neighborhood and would drag me along with him. It wasn't something I was interested in, but I came along with him. His uncle decided to take him storm chasing one day so Jeremy could see a real tornado.

I started getting into photography when I was twelve, and I started photographing the storms we chase. Capturing the sky through the lens of my camera is what made me want to keep chasing, even when I didn't like it as much."

"Ah, the classic storm chasing movie," Jonah picks up his glass of Coke. "I remember Jeremy calling me up one day and told me to watch it. Storms was something we shared a passion with while growing up, and my dad is a storm spotter. The movie is what got us hooked on wanting to become meteorologists." He takes a sip of his drink.

"I know, right?" Owen says. "Sawyer and I watched it and me are like 'We can make a career chasing storms?'"

"And that's exactly what we ended up doing," Sawyer adds. "We saw that movie when we were sixteen, and we had just gotten our license, so we went out to chase thunderstorms around our area in Nebraska. Our mother would have killed us if we had chased tornadoes. Even now that we are in college, she doesn't like the idea of us chasing them."

"Mind you, we have always lived in Tornado Alley, but never saw a tornado. Even when we had warnings, we never had one hit our town. Not until we moved to Oklahoma to study meteorology."

I listen to them as they talk about their experiences with tornadoes, and how they have gotten into chasing. Even if I didn't want to think about Jeremy, I couldn't help but imagine him sitting at this table and joining in on the stories about tornadoes.

Lindy shares her story next. She grew up in New York until she moved to Kansas where her mother and her lived with her grandmother, who lived on the plains. It was right before her mother met and married Jonah's dad. One summer in her teens there was a tornado that went through her grandmother's town. It had missed her grandmother's house, but when she saw the tornado for the first time, she became fascinated by them.

Jeremy would have love sitting amongst this table and chatting everything tornadoes, I think to myself as this wave of sadness hits me. It's not what I want to think about as I sit here eating my dinner and getting to know these people, who I will be spending this week with until it was time for me to go home. When I'm done with this chase Jeremy wanted me to do, I really don't know if I will continue chasing, or it's something I will do every now and again. Storm chasing is just not the same without him.

Back at the motel, Lindy takes a shower while I took the opportunity to call my brother liked I had promise him I would. I Facetime him as I sit down on the bed, the television playing softly in the background.

"Did you see a tornado today?" Avery asks me. He's sitting on the living room couch.

"Only briefly," I answer. "It was rain wrapped, and we could only just see it. We couldn't get to it as the area we were chasing in didn't have many paved roads, and driving onto dirt roads wasn't an option as they turned to mud from the rain."

"What's rain wrapped?"

I explain to him what it was.

"I'm glad you're safe, Anna. I was worried about you."

I give my brother a small smile. "Hey, buddy, you don't need to be worried. I'm going to be okay. I promise."

Avery doesn't look convince. He looks over his shoulder at something, perhaps to check where our parents were before he turns back to the camera.

"It's just every time I hear on the news about a tornado, I keep thinking about that day," he tells me. "When we had that thunderstorm the other night, I was so sure the tornado was going to come back."

I wish I could pull my arms through the camera and hug him tightly.

"I think about that day too," I say. "It was more terrifying than what I experience storm chasing. I mean, yeah, I do get scared when I chase, but at the same time there's this sense of thrilling adventure when you chase them. Tornadoes are unpredictable, and you never know what is going to happen. You just have to keep yourself safe when chasing them."

"Jeremy and his uncle weren't safe. I'm scared you will end up like them, Anna."

There's a brief silence between us as soon as my brother drops this on me. I still don't know exactly what happened to Jeremy and his uncle. Maybe they got too close, or maybe they were in the circulation and weren't aware of how close they were. I'm just never going to know. Chris's video camera that was on his dashboard was never found, neither was Jeremy's phone where I knew he would have filmed the chase. Perhaps the footage would reveal what happened. Or even if it was found, and Jeremy's parents got a hold of it, I'm not sure I want to know what happened to my best friend and his uncle.

I think back to this morning when Avery asked me why I was going chasing after everything that happened.

"Avery, do you remember what I said to you this morning?"

He nods. "Yes. You said you will come home."

I smile. "That's exactly what I'm going to do, Avery. I'm going to come home. This is something I need to do for Jeremy that he wanted both of us to do. As much as I want to stay away from chasing and not see another tornado, I can't stop thinking about Jeremy. I can't stop thinking about how there's something terrifying, yet fascinating about these storms. Jeremy wanted to learn everything there is to do about them. While Jeremy liked to study the science side of the storms, I like to photograph them."

"What are you going to do with the photos?"

"Upload them to my computer and share them online. I also want to collect some photos to add to my portfolio for college. Jeremy wants me to sell my pictures also, but that's something I don't know yet."

"You should. You take excellent photos, Anna."

I chatted to my brother for a bit longer before Mom and Dad come into view to say hello. I tell them about the day, and promise to talk to them tomorrow before hanging up the phone.

The shower cuts off. I grab the remote control to put the volume up when my phone rings. Dropping the remote, I see Moxie's name on the screen and answer.

"Hey, Moxie."

"Hey. How did it go today?"

I fill her in with today's events.

"That sucks. Do you think you have better luck tomorrow in seeing one?" she asks.

"Hopefully. There are a few storms happening in the centre of Tornado Alley that we are going to check out."

"How did you feel today when you were out chasing?"

"It feels strange without Jeremy, but it felt good to be out here. Thank you, Moxie, for encouraging me to come on this chase. I can't help but wonder what it would be like if Jeremy was here with me."

"He will be talking non-stop about the chase and how amazing the tornado is. Yeah right, Jeremy. There's nothing amazing about a tornado."

There's a sudden silence that falls between us when she says it. Now that Jeremy was no longer here, talking about storms was something I couldn't do with Moxie. She wasn't interested in anything weather. Every time we would speak about our adventures around her, she would always tell us we were insane. Maybe we were, but there's no denying the adrenalin rush when you chase tornadoes.

But even if Moxie wasn't into storms and it was something I couldn't talk to her about, I was glad she encouraged me to come along on this chase.

Yes, tornadoes are deadly, and there's nothing amazing about them when they cause major destruction. But there's this beauty side of them when they are just out there in the middle of nowhere, like in a field, far from anything they can destroy. The way they form and move is fascinating. When they form, you have no idea what kind of shape or size they are going to be. Sometimes I'm not even sure how to describe the feeling of seeing a tornado. There's this thrilling thing about seeing them, like this one in a life time event that you never know when you will see. Growing up, I had practice tornado drills in school, and hid in the basement when the sirens went off, but never actually seeing a tornado. That day when Jeremy and I chased our first storm together was the first time I saw a funnel cloud. At that time, I wasn't enthusiastic about it, not until Jeremy invited me out for our first chase with his uncle. Just seeing it in the distance was amazing. I started getting into photography because I wanted to capture the moment.

Though, chasing tornadoes and having one come towards

you are two different things. On a chase you can guarantee you will be safe if you keep a distance. But when you are in the path of one, you have no idea if the twister will be the last thing you will ever see.

Sometimes when I'm alone, and I'm thinking about what happened to Jeremy and his uncle, I think about our last chase day together. I kept wondering what would have happened if something had gone wrong. We had skipped school. Our parents didn't think we were anywhere except school. We were forbidden to chase on our own, not until we were eighteen which won't be until this summer. I can't imagine what my parents would feel if anything had happened that day. I'm thankful we were safe and had come home in one piece.

I just wish the same thing would have had happened that day. I wish Jeremy and his uncle came home in one piece. I wish they were here on this chase with Jeremy's cousins. He would be having the time of his life.

"Yeah," is all I can say in a soft voice, unsure how to respond to Moxie.

"How do you feel, Anna?" Moxie wants to know. "Do you feel good about being on the chase?"

I smile as I nod even if Moxie couldn't see it. We didn't video chat much because she didn't like it. "I feel good. It feels good to be out here. It doesn't feel the same without Jeremy though."

I picture Moxie smiling at the other end. "I'm glad, Anna. Even if you said you didn't want to chase without him, I'm glad you took this opportunity. I'm sure Jeremy would be watching you, smiling and cheering you on."

"I have you to thank for, Moxie. I wouldn't be here if it wasn't for you to convince me. I would be still at home, being miserable."

"Do you think you will chase next tornado season when you are in college?"

I shrug. That wasn't a decision I have made yet. "I don't know. Maybe. I could decide this is my last chase. I mean, storm chasing is a thing Jeremy and I did together. I'm on this chase because Jeremy organized this with his cousins. Jonah and Lindy are giving me an awesome opportunity to get up close to a tornado, which will be something I will be able to take excellent photos of. Not only do I get to take pictures, but for the first time I get to be involve with intercepting, helping to collect data, which is something Chris never did. He was happy viewing them from the distance. We most likely wouldn't do the science side until Jeremy got his degree. But I'm not sure if this is something I want to keep doing."

"I'm not going to tell you what you should do, but it's all up to you. I may not be into weather, but is storm chasing something you would have always end up doing with Jeremy, even after you go to college and have your own future? I swear when you guys spoke about the weather, there's always this smile on your face. Why did you think I suggested for you guys to date? You shared this hobby and you were always happy when you were together. Who are you, Anna, if you didn't chase? With or without Jeremy?"

A wave of sadness hits me as I think back to that day where the world ended for me. The conversation we had at lunch earlier that day when she thought it would have been a great idea for us to date. Maybe Jeremy and I would have been perfect for each other, make a living of chasing storms, documenting and studying them. Maybe love would have come later when we at least expected it.

But it didn't matter what Moxie wanted for us anymore.

And Moxie is right. Who am I if I didn't chase, and is it something I would do without Jeremy? It was his idea to start chasing. If it wasn't for him, I wouldn't have gotten into photography.

"It was nice to hear from you, but I think I'm going to call it a night," I say. "It's been a long day and I'm tired."

Moxie must have sense what I'm thinking. "Anna, I didn't mean to upset you."

"I'm not upset, Moxie. I just… Jeremy and I was never going to be together. We weren't interested in each other like that. It's not like it even matters anymore."

"I know. I only want you to be happy, Anna."

I know Moxie wanted me to be happy. Maybe Jeremy was the guy for me. But I never thought of dating someone who was into storm chasing. It was only a hobby I wanted to share with Jeremy. Even when he had talked about making discovers that could help scientists understand tornadoes better, I wanted to be on those chases with him. Not with anyone else.

"I know, Moxie. Goodnight."

She says goodnight and I hang up.

Once off the phone, I open up the gallery and stare at the final photo I had of Jeremy.

"Everything alright?"

I look up to see Lindy walking out of the bathroom, where she has changed into her pyjamas. She dries her hair with a towel.

I nod, setting my phone down beside me on the covers. "Yeah, I'm fine."

Lindy sits down on the bed next to me. "If you ever need to talk about something, Anna, you can talk to me. I have lost

Jeremy too, so I know what you're feeling."

I give her a small smile. "When I feel ready, I will. I don't want to talk about him right now."

Setting my phone down on the bedside table, I decided to call it a night. I don't even change out of my clothes as I go under the covers.

Jeremy, I wish you were here.

Chapter 12

I dream about him that night. I dream about us chasing tornadoes, getting up close to them, trying to figure out how tornadoes work. Maybe it was because it was the last thing Moxie and I talk about, but we kissed. We had chased a storm, and when it dissipated, Jeremy kisses me. It was short and sweet.

It's 4am when I wake up, lying in the darkness with this strange feeling of sadness in my chest. Perhaps it was to do with the dream or if the dream felt real like Jeremy was here. Or maybe I was missing out on something I will never know what would happen if it did.

I try to go back to sleep, but I wasn't able to. I thought of taking a walk around the motel, but I didn't want to wake anyone up. It didn't matter anyway, because Lindy's alarm went off an hour later.

Around seven, we place our belongings in the vehicles before going out for breakfast at the diner we were at last night.

While we wait for our food, Jonah has his laptop open to the weather radar. Like he had mentioned yesterday, there were possible storm cells building up around Kansas and Oklahoma. The chasers talk weather terms that I only understand briefly from Jeremy, discussing which storm fonts they should follow that had a high chance of producing a tornado. They decide on the Kansas storm.

But before we could head off on the long journey, we had to stop at the repair shop to fix the damage windshield.

While we waited, I find a message from Moxie.

I hope we are still good about what I said last night. I'm sorry if I upset you.

I start typing a message, wanting to so badly tell her about my dream last night, but I decided to keep it to myself. So instead, I write **We are all good and don't worry about it.** I add a thumbs up emoji.

I pull out the photo of Jeremy and I again on our last chase.

I stare at it for a long time before saying, "I'm going to make you proud, Jeremy. I'm going to try and do this chase without you, even if it seems hard."

* * *

We are out on the Great Plains in Kansas. It's mid-afternoon and the clouds are building up. While the team studies the clouds and where to go to next, I take pictures of the sky and the landscape.

Jonah stands beside me. "How did you start getting into

photography?"

"When I first started going on chases with Jeremy, I just thought that the formation of the clouds was amazing. It made me want to capture it and remember the chases."

"And you went on one chase, now it's something you need to do every time," Jonah adds.

I nod, smiling. He knows exactly how it felt once you get a taste of chasing. "You could say that. I mean, I didn't want to go chasing at first, and thought you had to be crazy to chase tornadoes. I always thought tornadoes were scary, and of course they are up close, but when you view them from the distance, they are amazing. We saw a tornado on our first chase, and when I saw it for the first time, the fear I had always had from seeing them on TV disappeared. Seeing it up close was like a whole new perspective on how I view them. They are just so amazing, Jonah. I will admit, though, that if Jeremy never asked me to come storm chasing, I wouldn't have gotten into photography. There's this peace of mind I have whenever I capture stormy weather."

"Tornadoes are amazing. I started out going on chases with Dad. He's a storm spotter. And then I started chasing with my Uncle Chris. Some days he chased with Jeremy, then he would chase with me, and sometimes he chased with the both of us. Since Jeremy encouraged me to chase them, it became a career I didn't think I would end up doing. Seeing a tornado is scary and thrilling all at the same time."

"My little brother is wondering how can I chase after what we went through." I shrug. "I don't know. I mean, like you said. It's an addiction. At first, I wasn't going to chase anymore after Jeremy passed, but my other friend convinced me to take on this opportunity. This chase is a special one – for Chris and

Jeremy. I guess I couldn't turn you down for it."

"You could if you wanted to. No one is forcing you here."

"I know, but Jeremy wouldn't want me to. We had always chase for fun to learn more about tornadoes. I photographed the storms, and Jeremy studied the science side of them."

"Are you going to keep chasing after this week?"

I shrug. "I don't know yet."

"I hope you do." He gestures to my camera around my neck. "I bet you have taken many great photos of storms."

I nod, smiling. "I have. After my first tornado, I wanted to take pictures. I didn't have a camera, so on my next chase, Jeremy surprised me with one. At the time money was tight so my parents couldn't buy me a camera. Jeremy brought me this camera he half brought with his pocket money and with the help of his parents. Once I started taking pictures of storms on our chases, I fell in love with photography."

"Awesome. Is it possible I could see some of them?"

I direct him to my Instagram page, and he promises to take a look at it later.

Lindy turns to us. "I'm thinking of heading south of the storm. Is that alright with you, Jonah?"

Jonah looks up at the sky before nodding, turning back to Lindy. "Yes, let's head south."

Getting back in the vehicles, we head south. The county we are in has a tornado watch, so we knew we were in the right location. Hopefully we will be able to get up close and see a tornado this time.

Lindy drives, and Jonah sits in the back with me, looking at my Instagram.

"These pictures are fantastic," Jonah says. "You have a great eye."

I smile at him. "Thanks."

"Have you ever consider selling these photographs?"

I shake my head. "Jeremy suggested I should, but I don't know. I'm studying photography at college in the fall, but I'm not sure what career path I will take."

"Whatever pictures you take when you storm chase with us, you should definitely sell the pictures to the media. Someone out there will love your work."

"I will definitely keep that in mind."

Lindy drives several miles before she pulls over to the side road near a farm. A couple of storm chasers are also lined up on the side, observing the same storm.

Getting out, Sawyer grabs his drone to observe the storm from above. We were definitely in a better position of the storm than the one we had chased yesterday. The wind has picked up and the chasers are getting back into their vehicles as lightning began getting close. Jonah orders us to do the same so none of us get struck by lightning.

With the winds picking up, Sawyer has trouble getting his drone to come back down. He manages to get it down and then races to the car.

"Sawyer, did you pick anything up on your drone to indicate this storm could produce a tornado?" Lindy asks.

"Over on the south west of the storm there's a lot of rotation in the clouds," Sawyer explains.

"Right, let's get moving in that direction, shall we?"

Lindy turns onto the road, heading south west.

I stare out the window, watching the sky, keeping an eye out for a wall cloud. They move fast across the sky, making the afternoon seem like night. Lightning flashes across the sky and thunder rumbles. Sawyer is right about the clouds rotating.

I can see them as we move along the road. We are definitely getting a tornado. I can feel it.

"Hey, over to the right there's a wall cloud!" Jonah points out.

I glance in Jonah's direction and surely enough in the field next to us is the base of one. Lindy pulls to the side. A few other chasers have also pull over to capture a glimpse of the wall cloud.

Getting out, I get my camera ready while the others talk weather terms. I snap away. I even capture a picture of Jonah with his back to me as he stares at the sky. The way he stands there, his hands on his hips reminded me of Jeremy when he is observing a storm.

I put my camera down for a second, letting it sit on my chest as it dangles on the strap. I watch Jonah carefully as his eyes is everywhere, focusing on the sky above us. Just like how Jeremy was.

When he turns around to face me, I quickly grab my camera, holding it in my hands so he would think I was taking photos and not standing there staring at him.

"Are you getting great pictures?" he asks, walking over to me.

I nod. "I am."

"Promise to show them to me later?"

I smile. "I will."

He stands beside me, his arm brushing up against me as he points towards the wall cloud. "It's rotating a lot over there." He turns to me with a smile. "It looks like we could get a tornado."

I see the rotation. I zoom the camera up onto it. I can practically hear Jeremy cheering excitedly that the chance of a tornado is going to happen. There's a lot of lightning within this supercell thunderstorm.

"Do you think we might get any hail from this storm?" I ask Jonah.

"We might." Jonah points out some green in the clouds. "Definitely this is a severe thunderstorm."

The sky grows darker, turning the sky to dusk.

"Lindy, Jonah, a hook echo is forming on the radar," Owen announces.

"Excellent," Jonah says. "I have a good feeling about this storm."

Some chasers get into their vehicles to get a view of the potential tornado from another spot. We stay where we are, which Jonah reckons we won't be hit by hail this time. He didn't want to risk losing another windshield after replacing the last one.

"There!" Jonah shuts, pointing over at the wall cloud. "A funnel is forming!"

Owen is filming it. "Yes, we are going to get a tornado!"

I get my camera ready, waiting to snap it as soon as the funnel touches the ground. As soon as I see the debris cloud, I snap a photo of it.

"The tornado is on the ground!" Sawyer calls out as his brother continues filming it, commenting on what a beautiful tornado it is.

Lindy is on the phone to call in the tornado. Seconds after getting off, an alert is coming from our phones and the car radio, warning us about the tornado on the ground.

We stand there for a few minutes, watching it before we realize the tornado is heading towards us. We have a few minutes to move before it hits us, so Jonah suggested to drop a probe right here. With the help of Lindy and Sawyer, they help

Jonah to get the probe out of the SUV, setting it down on the side of the road. Then we scramble into the vehicle, speeding up the road where the other chasers headed.

We pull over on the side of the road as the tornado crosses the road. Getting out of the car, Owen continued filming the tornado.

The stovepipe vortex was beautiful with the debris cloud surrounding it. I haven't been this close to a whirlwind since that day my life changed forever. At the back of my mind, I tell myself I needed to get out of here, get somewhere safe, that I can't be this close to a tornado after what happened two weeks ago. But I argue with my conscious that I can stand here, observing the storm like I have always done. It was a whole different feeling standing here, watching it move across the road than when I had come face to face with it coming towards me. I smile as I capture a perfect picture of it.

"Did you capture it, Anna?" I imagine what Jeremy would say if he was here.

"I did."

"Isn't this tornado beautiful?"

Once the tornado passes the road, heading into the field on the other side, Jonah and I rush over to the fence that has been dismantled. There's a farm house in the distance and I hope the people are in a safe place, and that the tornado spares them.

"Did you get any awesome shots?" Jonah beams, the excitement in his voice.

"I did. I can't wait to see the shots later. I have never gotten this close to a tornado on a chase before. I can just imagine Jeremy being over the moon right now."

Owen comes over to us, filming the tornado. Behind us,

Lindy is asking everyone if they know if the tornado has gone over the probe. There isn't any certainly if it has, but I'm sure it was able to capture the data they needed.

"Let's get back in the car and see if we can catch up to it."

Before I follow the others in the car, I watch the tornado. Glancing up at the sky above me, I say, "Thank you, Jeremy, for this amazing opportunity."

Chapter 13

We catch up to the tornado. It narrowly dodges the small town, but destroys a few farms that are out on the plains. Jonah and Lindy manage to place another probe in its path, which Jonah brags about what data they will be able to capture.

Ending the chase for the day, we headed off to find a motel for the night once we helped out nearby properties that were damaged. Thankfully only a few homes were destroyed and that the twister doesn't go through the town. No one was hurt and that's a good thing.

I share a room with Lindy again. While she talks on the phone with her boyfriend, who also chases and is currently doing an internship and wasn't able to chase with us, I uploaded the pictures I had taken onto my laptop. The close up photos I had taken of the tornado when it cross the road came out so good. I sent the photo to Jonah through Messenger so he could see the results.

He replies back in seconds. **Great shots.**

I know! I can't believe how great it turned out.

This will make an excellent front page cover of a magazine.

I picture it for a second and he is right. It would make an excellent front page cover for a magazine.

I pull up the photo I took with Jonah looking out at the wall cloud, his hands on his hips. I haven't told him I had taken the picture of him, but it really did remind me of Jeremy.

I sent the photo to Moxie. **This photo I took today reminds me so much of Jeremy when he is storm watching.**

I expected Moxie to message back, but instead she calls me.

I answer just as Lindy gets off the phone and told me she was going over to see the guys, and will be back soon.

"Hey, Moxie," I say as soon as Lindy closes the door.

"Hey, how was it out there today?"

"It was great. The good thing is the tornado wasn't rain wrapped today, and we were able to see it. We also managed to put two probes out in the path of it to collect data."

"That's good. Are you chasing tomorrow?"

"I'm not sure yet. I haven't checked the weather."

"I like the picture you sent me. After last night, I didn't expect to hear from you."

"Hey, I told you I wasn't upset. And I know you want me to be with Jeremy, or even someone I storm chase with. The truth is, I haven't decided if I will keep chasing. This could be the last chase."

"Are you sure, Anna? I don't want you to be unhappy

because you stopped chasing. Even if Jeremy isn't here, I'm sure he would want you to keep chasing no matter what. This photo you sent me is amazing, and I'm sure you have taken many more. You could be a great storm photographer. You capture so many amazing shots that not many people get to take. Not just with tornadoes, but with thunderstorms as well."

I think about what Moxie said, and it's something I have never thought about before. Is this something Jeremy wanted me to do when he invited me along with his cousins, to get closer to tornadoes than we have had on other chases? I don't want to be a meteorologist, but perhaps Chris and Jeremy saw me being able to pursue a different path to storm chasing where I could photograph storms instead of studying them. As a kid I used to be terrified of storms. The sound of the thunder made me want to hide, even when Jeremy wanted me to come outside to observed the storm. But when I wasn't until the first chase that I saw a different side of the storms that made me want to photograph them. Seeing a bolt of lightning ripping across the sky, or a funnel cloud touching the ground, was like seeing an untold story that made me want to capture it through the lens of a camera. Could I even give it up all because my best friend had died and wouldn't lead the chases?

I don't know. But snapping landscapes didn't have the same feel as when I'm photographing storms. There's this excitement when a bolt of lightning flashes across the sky and that rumble of thunder that makes me wonder what is the sky going to do next.

"I will see what happens when this chase ends," I say.

"Okay. Remember, I'm not telling you what you should do, but I just want you to be happy."

"I know you do."

"So tell me, who is that in the photo you sent me? Is that Jonah?"

I nod. "It is."

"How is it going with him?"

"Good, I guess. I really like this photo I took of him. The way he observes the storm reminds me of Jeremy."

"You like him." I imagine her grinning on the other end of the phone.

"What?" I have known Jonah for a few days, even though I had met him a few years ago for the wedding, but this was the most I have spent time with him. Yeah, he is cute, but I don't like him. Besides, he's Jeremy's cousin. I don't think he would want me dating his cousin.

"You like him," Moxie repeats.

I was so thankful Lindy wasn't in the room right now. I'm sure my cheeks are a bright red. What would she say if she had overheard Moxie saying I may possibly like her stepbrother?

"No, I do not."

"Anna, I think you do like him, but you don't know it yet."

I roll my eyes. "Moxie, we have only known each other for a few days. Besides, I'm sure we won't keep in contact after the weekend."

"Why not?"

I shrug. "Well, for one, he's Jeremy's cousin. I don't think he would like me crushing on him. Second, I'm sure he has no interest in me."

"Don't be silly, Anna. You won't know until you give it a try. I'm sure Jeremy wouldn't mind you dating his cousin."

I roll my eyes. Whatever Moxie wants to believe, she can believe it because it's not going to happen. I wasn't interested in anyone. I just want to move on from Jeremy's death, go off to do the things I told him I dreamed of doing. My main goal in life was to have a career as a photographer. I don't know what path I will take yet, but I hope to find out once I start college in the fall.

A knock comes from the door. It's probably Lindy. She must have forgotten her key.

"I got to go, Moxie," I say, getting off the bed. "I will call you later."

I open the door expecting to see Lindy, but instead it was Jonah standing at the door.

I smile. "Hey. What can I do for you?"

"Hey, so there's a thunderstorm coming in and I was just wondering if you would like to come out to watch it? Maybe you could take some photos."

"Sure. I would love to. I love thunderstorms at night."

"I know, right? They put on a spectacular light show."

I grab my camera, as well as the key to the room. We were on the second floor of the motel. Outside of our room in the distance is a storm brewing in. There's a slight sound of thunder and lightning bolts ripping up the sky.

"The storm isn't a tornadic supercell?"

He shakes his head. "No. I wouldn't be getting you out here if it was. We would most likely be getting into the car right now to chase it. We haven't done a night chase for a while, but it's something we want to do again. We have done a night chase once when we team up with some professional storm chasers."

I point my camera towards the lightning storm, waiting for the perfect moment to capture the lightning. I couldn't wait for the storm to get closer and get close ups.

Jonah and I watch the storm in silence. Watching the storm with him made me think of all the times I would observe thunderstorms rolling in with Jeremy.

"When I was younger, Jeremy would always make me come outside to watch storms," I break the silence. "Sometimes at night, he would sneak into my room so we could watch the lightning. If a siren ever went off, instead of seeking shelter like I told him we should do, he wanted to get out there on his bike to see if he could get a glimpse of a funnel. We didn't go very far from our house in case we need to seek shelter. We only ever saw a funnel once on the outskirts of our town."

Jonah chuckles. "I remember when Jeremy did that too. When he came to visit sometimes, where my parents were married before they divorced, my mom had a hard time trying to get him to come inside whenever there was a storm. During one summer when he stayed with us, we had a tornado warning, and the sirens were going off, he was out in the backyard observing the clouds. My mom would be screaming at him to get into the basement while being on the phone at the same time to his mom, telling him he won't get in the basement. Then when my aunt couldn't get him in the basement, Mom would be on the phone to my dad who was a storm spotter for the weather station, trying to get my dad to tell him to get inside. It never worked of course. But Jeremy made sure he was safe, and if there was any sign of danger, then he would get inside."

I loved it how Jonah and I could share stories about Jeremy, our memories of him whenever it came to storms. Maybe I couldn't talk with Moxie about storms, but if I do end up staying in contact with Jeremy's cousins, I had Jonah to talk to.

I snap a few shots of a lightning strike ripping across the sky. If Jeremy was here, he will be staring at the sky in awe, saying things like 'Will you look at that!' or 'Look how amazing that is!'

"When this week is over, do you think you might come chasing with us again?" Jonah asks me. "I mean, I know you were meant to come chasing next month, but you ended up coming early. You are still welcome to come chasing next month."

I watch the lightning as I hold onto my camera without looking at Jonah. The thunder sounds like it's getting louder, and it won't be long until it reaches us.

How do I tell Jonah that after this chase, I'm not sure if I want to continue chasing without Jeremy? I know Moxie and I had discussed that I should, that Jeremy wouldn't want me to miss out on chasing with his cousins. Right now, I don't know what I want. Maybe it's something I won't decide until March next year when storm season starts again.

"I don't know what I want to do yet," I tell him. "I don't know if I want to continue chasing without Jeremy."

Jonah turns his body towards me. "But why stop when he's gone?"

He had a point. And like Moxie had said, this was our thing. Something we did together that made us happy. Taking the opportunity to work with his cousins and their friends has been great. I have learned a whole different side of chasing, something I wasn't going to get to do until we reach college, where we no longer had to have his uncle with us and we could go chasing ourselves.

But no one here understands what I'm really feeling. There's this empty hole inside me without Jeremy. I can't share the excitement of a chase with anyone like I could with him. Moxie doesn't care about the weather, so sharing everything about tornadoes with her is not going to happen. I could talk with Jonah and Lindy, as they will understand how I felt, but I didn't know them well enough to talk to them about anything.

I force myself to look at Jonah. "These past two weeks has been hard without him. Storm chasing was a hobby we did together. Without him, it feels… empty."

Jonah nods slowly, not taking his eyes off me. "I understand, Anna. It hasn't been easy for my family either since my Uncle Chris and Jeremy were killed. But I do know one thing: Jeremy wouldn't want you to give up on chasing just because he is gone. The photos you showed me, Anna, are fantastic. You make an excellent storm photographer. I mean, you probably won't get this many great shots if you sit at home. You're getting these great shots of storms because of these chases. You and Jeremy shared a hobby together, with two different passions in mind. His passion was to chase the storms and study them, while yours is to photograph them."

I smile, remembering the first chase we did with his uncle, how I wanted to photograph the tornado we had seen. The rotating column air was so fascinating, despite the fear I had always had of ever coming across them, the fear turned to fascination. I wanted to photograph them. I wanted to capture every movement they made.

"I'm still trying to figure out what I want. I know Moxie thinks I should. It's just that no one really understands how Jeremy and I bonded over storm chasing. Don't get me wrong, but I do like being on this chase with you guys. It's just it feels lonely without Jeremy."

Jonah nods his head slowly. "I get it. I can't imagine never not chasing with Lindy or any of my friends. Sometimes I go out on chases with my dad. I come from a family who are weather enthusiasts. My dad works with the news network and storm spots. Before I started doing a few chases with my Uncle Chris and Jeremy, I went on a few chases with my dad as a kid, curious at what he does. I wanted to see if it was anything like *Twister*. The first time I chased with him, I just knew it was what I was going to do as a life time career. I'm sure after I graduate from college with my degree that I may have my own team, and won't chase with Dad, or Lindy or any of my friends. For now, I like it where I am and what I'm doing."

I think about what he had said, letting it sink in. Jeremy and I never spoke about what would have happened after college. He had talked about still chasing storms together, but never if we decide to go our separate ways. I imagine it would have been me, taking a different path in my photography that wouldn't allow me to drive across Tornado and Dixie Alley in hope to photograph a tornado. We rarely chased in Dixie Alley, but there's a few times we have. The mid-west is where we liked to chase the most than the south, mostly because Dixie Alley often has poor visibility for tornadoes, where they are often hidden behind trees, making it dangerous to spot them.

Or maybe we never discussed it because we never had to feel that our chasing days together could come to an end.

Even when we will go our separate ways, I imagine Jeremy calling me up to come out with him. If we had kids, maybe we would bring them along.

"Can you promise me something, Anna?" Jonah says when I don't respond to his last comment.

"I can't guarantee that I will, but I can try."

"Promise me you will come back for the summer to chase. At least then decide if you want to continue chasing for next season. You are probably deciding not to chase because you're mourning Jeremy, so your mind isn't clear enough to make any proper decisions. I think when you completely feel like you have moved on, you will make the right decision to what you want to do."

I never thought of it like that. I guess there is no harm in chasing over the summer one last time.

I nod. "Okay. I will continue chasing over the summer with you before I make the decision that I want."

Jonah smiles. "I look forward to doing more chases with you."

Chapter 14

The next morning, we head southeast towards Kansas, Oklahoma and Missouri, where the borders meet. There were several supercells predicted across the mid-west today. The one near the borders was just one of the storms we will be chasing today.

Reaching the Kansas/Oklahoma border, we pull over to observe the clouds building up, getting a sense of which direction we should head in. Jonah decided to move the team across the border to Oklahoma. He predicted the storm will develop in Oklahoma, and move northeast to Missouri.

The clouds grow darker when we are a couple of miles south of the border. Thunder rumbles as the storm gets closer. The storm produces a lot of amazing lightning strikes, and I take some shots of them.

Jonah and the others study the clouds, talking in weather terms I don't understand. Not only did they study the clouds, they study the radar to where a tornado was mostly likely to form. Lindy wanted another shot with the probes. The tornado from yesterday had slightly missed the probes we placed in the path of it.

Hail soon falls, and while we all escaped into the vehicle, Owen is the only one who is brave enough to stand out there. He has on a helmet as he collected the baseball size hail, to take measurements of the hail stones. He curses a few times when he had gotten hit by them. Thankfully the hail doesn't smash the windshield this time.

After the hail hits, it was like it had snowed. It looked spectacular and I had to take a photo of it.

Moving south of the storm, a wall cloud begins to form. The air is still, one sign we are going to get a tornado. The feeling is scary at first because we have no idea what is going to happen, but at the same time it's exciting not knowing what kind of funnel cloud we will see.

I glance around at my surroundings, wondering where a tornado could most likely form, and where it might travel to. We were in a rural area, and there were only two properties I could see along the road. Hopefully the tornado will spare them. There's a small town half a mile from here, and I can only hope it will miss the town.

It starts to rain, and that's when we see a funnel.

"Funnel!" Sawyer cries out as he and his brother aims their video cameras at it. "We have a funnel!"

Lindy gets onto the phone to call in the funnel. We have no idea where this tornado will go, but hopefully there will be enough warning for people to take cover.

The funnel cloud reaches the ground in seconds. It's a wedge, smaller than the wedge tornado that almost wiped out Brooke's Creek.

"Another tornado!" Jonah points out. "It's a multi-vortex."

At first, I don't see it, but then I see a second vortex dancing around the main vortex.

"Anna, are you getting this?" Jonah asks me.

Of course, I am. I'm snapping as many photos as I could in case it disappears. I imagine Jeremy here. He has always found the multi-vortex tornadoes fascinating and I could just imagine how excited he would be to view it, capturing it on his camera.

The tornado moves across the field, heading towards the properties up ahead. We scramble back into the car, taking off after it. Thankfully the tornado misses the farm houses and barns, going around the back of the properties.

It then starts to shift left, heading towards us. We slow down, not wanting to get into the path. Jonah thought that maybe he had enough time to jump out and drop a probe, but then we notice cars zooming pass us in hope to get pass before the tornado crosses the road. Or maybe they were unaware the funnel was heading towards the road.

Jonah curses. "Those people are going to get themselves killed if they don't stop."

Making sure we are at a safe position, Jonah gets out of the vehicle, standing on the road to wave down motorists who were trying to attempt to get past the tornado, while trying not to get knocked off his feet from the strong winds. He slows two cars coming along, yelling that there is a tornado coming towards us.

The tornado crosses the road. I get out of the car to capture the shot of the vortex in the middle of the road. With it being several metres in front of me, I stare at the vortex, watching it as it rotates. The way it moves was fascinating, especially with the smaller vortex around it. It was something I could stare at for hours if I had the chance to.

Getting back in the vehicle, we race after the tornado. Sawyer navigates the team on which road to take so we can get up ahead of the tornado. When we do, we have a few minutes to place a probe in its path and then get out of the way. Jonah and I keep an eye on the tornado as Owen, Sawyer and Lindy places a probe on the side of the road.

Racing to the car, we reverse down the road we had come from, watching as the tornado cross the road right where we were.

"Can you see if it has gone over the probe?" Lindy asks Owen who is at the wheel.

"It's too early to tell, but it looks like it might have."

Owen has to back up a bit as our vehicle was getting hit by debris, meaning we were too close.

The tornado moves across the road and into a corn field. There's a barn in the tornado's path just a few meters from where it's ripping up the corn, and from the looks of it, it's going to hit the barn head on.

Lindy is the first to jump out of the vehicle once it was safe to do so, and runs over to where we had placed the probe. The rest of us get out, following Lindy. Sawyer keeps his camera on the vortex, continuing to film.

I wanted to join the others near the probe, but I stand a short distance from Sawyer, mesmerized by the whirling vortex. It has reached the barn, and I watch it rip the building apart within seconds.

"Hey, give me your camera for a second," Jonah says with his hand out.

I hand it over to him, and he takes it, instructing me to look back at the tornado. I do as he asks, my back to him, the vortex now further away from us, heading towards the farm house after it tore up the barn and made a path through the corn field. I wasn't sure if we were going to keep chasing it once we retrieve the probe.

"That looks fantastic," Jonah says.

I glance over my shoulder. "What does?"

He presses something on my camera and turns it around so I can see what he had taken. He took a picture of me facing the tornado. The picture looked so cool with my back to the camera. I have never gotten a picture like this before. I have a similar photo I had taken of Jeremy, but there was none of me.

I take the camera from Jonah. "It looks great, Jonah. Thank you so much."

He smiles. "When you're deciding if you should keep storm chasing, all you need to do is look at this picture. You can't see your face, but when I took this, I just knew how much you enjoy being out here. Jeremy may not be here, yet you are doing something you both loved doing together. You wouldn't be here if you didn't enjoy storm chasing – with or without Jeremy."

We stare at each other for what feels like a long time. Butterflies dance around my stomach as I take notice of how close we were standing to each other. What he said is something I haven't thought about before. Moxie may had convinced me to come out here with Jeremy's cousins and their team, knowing how passionate I was about my photography. If I wasn't passionate or I didn't enjoy it when Jeremy was alive, then I wouldn't be here. I would still be at home, mourning. Here, I am living Jeremy's dreams and relieving something we have done together for so long.

Jonah breaks eye contact first and joins his stepsister and friends across the road. I watch Jonah and his team excitedly talk about the tornado and what data they could have capture on the probe. I then glance back at the tornado. It's far in the distance now.

This is what drew Jeremy to storm chasing. It wasn't about getting up close to a tornado or thrill-seeking adventures. It was about following what is your passion. It was also learning something that no one properly understood about tornadoes. There's something new to study each time and new data that maybe hasn't been already collected. Ongoing efforts that could improve warning systems. Perhaps someday they will be able to predict what supercells will form a tornado, or where it will mostly hit. There was so much to learn about these terrifying and powerful storms.

I glance down at the camera in my hands. I remember when Jeremy first gave it to me when we started chasing together.

Imagine what you could capture with it, Anna, he had said. *Especially when we go storm chasing together.*

I have not been on one storm chase without this camera. Every moment I had with it, I snapped pictures, wanting to remember everything. I wanted to capture the amazing storms and share it with others. I wanted to look back at them someday with my future kids, sharing stories about my chases.

Giving this all up will be crazy. Both Moxie and Jonah are right. Storm chasing is what drew Jeremy and I closer as friends. If I gave it all up, would I be happy? What's going to happen when I finish chasing with Jeremy's cousins and their friends, and I go back home?

"Jonah, Lindy, are we going to keep chasing this tornado?" Sawyer calls out, his camera focus on the tornado. "It's getting away fast. It looks like it's heading towards town."

Jonah looks over at the tornado. "Let's get this probe into the car, and continue chasing the storm."

Lindy and Owen helped Jonah carry the probe to the car. We then hop back in, racing towards the tornado. It narrowly misses the small town it comes across. The sirens are blaring loudly in the town. Some other storm chasers are also on the road.

When we were away from the town, the tornado tears through another corn field on someone's property and destroys a barn. I was glad it misses the house unlike it did with the other farm.

Jonah pulls over and we get out. Instead of photographing this time, I pull out my phone to record. I haven't filmed any twisters since my last chase with Jeremy. I steady the phone in my hand, the wind so strong that I thought it might knock me over.

I can almost hear Jeremy tell me how beautiful and amazing this tornado is.

The team and I manage to get the last of documenting the storm before it dissipated.

I stand there as the team cheers about the amazing chase, staring up at the clouds, smiling at myself as the rain continues.

"I wish you were here, Jeremy," I whisper loudly to myself. "You would have loved being here."

"How amazing was that tornado?" Sawyer says as I join the team. "Can you imagine what data we collected?"

"I can't wait to get to a motel and analyse it," Jonah says. He stares up at the sky before turning to us. "Awesome work today, team. Let's get going and head to Peterson for the night."

We start moving to the car when Lindy speaks.

"Hey, Jonah," she holds out her phone, "I know you want to settle down in Peterson for the night, but there is another supercell producing around that area. Possibly tornadoes."

Jonah takes the phone from Lindy to glance at the radar.

He nods. "Yes, it does look like there could possibly be tornadoes." He hands the phone back to Lindy.

She takes it. "Should we chase it? It's on the way to Peterson, and we could catch the second storm before we settle for the night."

Jonah thinks for a second. "Let's drive out there and see what we got before we call it a day."

Chapter 15

We drive west of Oklahoma, a few miles outside of Peterson. The clouds are darkening by the second, with a greenish color in them. We watch the lightning and wait for a wall cloud to develop, but there was nothing. Just a whole lot of lightning, thunder and rain. There was one moment where we were sure a funnel would be dropped, but then that disappeared.

As the sky darkens, an amazing sunset forms over the horizon. It turns the sky a bright orange and yellow, making the sky look amazing with the storm clouds. It was something I have never seen before, and it made a perfect photo opportunity.

Soon the sky turns to night, and out here in the plains, where we were a couple of miles out of the town Peterson, turns pitch black. Only the flashes of lightning gave us the light we needed to see. The storm hasn't produced a tornado, but it doesn't mean it won't. Our chase ends for the day. Owen asks about staying out a little longer, wanting to do a night chase, but there was nothing on the radar that says there will be a tornado tonight. Jonah had thought about it, but decided it was best to head to a motel for the night if there if the storm doesn't produce a tornado. The team was still inexperience with chasing at night, but if there was an opportunity, they wouldn't past it up. As I looked up at the stormy night sky, I pray silently that there would be an opportunity to do so, to experience what a night chase would be like. Chris never allowed us to night chase, and I understood why. It was dangerous and harder to spot a funnel. Jeremy had begged him a couple of times to do one, but he never gave in to his nephew.

Settling down at a motel for the night, we grab something to eat at the diner next door. The diner is quiet tonight with a few people sitting down to eat. A news broadcast was playing on the television on the corner of the left side of the diner at a low volume, discussing the storms for tonight and a tornado watch that's in effect until 9:00pm.

I slide into a booth next to Jonah, Lindy on the other side of him, and the brothers sat across. Jonah picks up the menu, and I glance at it. The brothers grab the other menu, and discuss it between each other, leaving Lindy to grab the last menu. The waitress comes by once we were ready to order our food and drinks.

The rain is really coming down outside. Watching the rain and listening to the thunder is relaxing. But hopefully it will slow down once we finish our dinner.

"So, Anna, how have you been enjoying the chase?" Sawyer

asks me.

I smile. "I have really enjoyed it. I hesitated for a long time if I wanted to take Jonah's offer after Jeremy died, and I'm glad I did. It has been great and I have learned a whole different side of chasing."

"What did you do before?" Owen wants to know.

I share a few stories about my chases.

"I haven't met Jeremy or Chris," Owen says. "It would have been totally awesome to have them both on the chase. Do share some of the photos you have taken. I would love to see them."

I direct him to my Instagram page. "I haven't posted any of the new chase photos I have taken this week, but I will probably do so once I upload them all onto my computer."

The brothers scroll through my Instagram.

"These photos are amazing," Sawyer says. "You really have a good eye for storm photography."

I smile as they hand my phone back. "Thanks."

Lindy's phone rings. She glances at her phone and asks Jonah and I to scoot across so she can get out to answer. She answers the phone and goes out near the door to talk. Lightning flashes across the sky as she walks outside, staying close to the shelter of the diner.

"Do you think this storm is going to end?" I ask.

Owen shakes his head. "It doesn't look like it's going to."

Sawyer looks up from where he had been glancing at his phone. "Guys, we have a problem."

"What kind of problem?" Jonah asks.

He shows us a short video from his phone. "My buddy just sent me this. He's out storm watching, and he sent me this video."

It's unclear what the video is, but when I look closer, I can just make out a funnel. Lightning lights up in the background, and it's the only way you could see it.

"Where is it at?" Owen asks. He grabs his phone from his pocket. "There's no tornado warning issue yet."

"Maybe they aren't aware of it just yet," Sawyer says.

"The tornado has been spotted out near Burke. That's the next town over from Peterson."

Lindy comes running into the diner. "Guys, we need to go. I have just gotten a call from a friend who is out chasing this storm. There's a tornado on the ground."

"The one out near Burke?" Sawyer asks. "Yes, I have gotten a text from my friend who has just informed me about it."

Lindy's eyes widen, shaking her head. "No. This one isn't in Burke. This one is over in Longdale. That's just west of here."

Sawyer curses. "We are in the centre of those towns."

"What? Do you think the storms could hit us?" Jonah wants to know.

Sawyer shrugs. "Maybe. Who knows what the storm could do."

Our phones began buzzing. We all check our phones to see we have a tornado warning for our area.

"Tornado warning," Lindy reads out loud.

We turn our attention to the TV next where an emergency broadcast is issue.

"A tornado has been confirmed in both Burke and Longdale, Oklahoma," the weather man says. "A tornado warning has been issued for the Hartley County, which includes Peterson, Rivervale, Ryde and Oakley, where the storms are predicted to hit next." He goes on to talk about tornado safety and what to do in case the tornado does hit our area.

A man in a plaid shirt and a blue baseball cap at a nearby table snickers, claiming there will be no tornado.

Pulling out our wallets, we drop dollar bills and coins in the centre of the table, feeling guilty that our food was being made, yet we can't eat it.

We reach our motel room. The guys and Lindy grab their cameras and laptops. I grab my camera also. We were chasing the storm, even though Jonah said they were inexperienced with chasing at night, but it was something the team wanted to get better at. We are right in the middle of it all, we might as well chase it.

"Sawyer, do you have a location to where the tornadoes are at?" Lindy wants to know as we pile our equipment into the car.

Sawyer doesn't answer until he climbs into the front passenger seat. Lindy gets behind the wheel while the rest of us pile in the back seat. "The one near Burke is at Highway 51. That's about twenty minutes from us, and it looks like it could be on a direct path through Peterson. The one in Longdale is heading north, so it won't hit us."

"What's the plan, Lindy?" Jonah asks.

"We are going to track this tornado," Lindy explains. "It's night. Not everyone will get the warning, especially when it's hard to spot the funnels at night. They may have sent out warnings for this area, but they might not set the sirens off unless the funnel is spotted heading towards town. We will see if we can spot the tornado and send out an alert if it does get closer to town."

Lindy turns onto the road, heading in the direction to where the tornado was last spotted. There was a lot of lightning so hopefully it will help us see the funnel. The only thing we were unsure about if the tornado is rain wrapped. We also look out for any power flashes.

"Any word from your friends to where the tornado could be?" Jonah asks Sawyer and Lindy.

Lindy shakes her head. "No, I haven't heard anything else."

"Me either," Sawyer adds.

I glance out the window, looking everywhere to see if I can spot any signs of a tornado approaching us. All I see is rain, pouring down heavily, a whole lot of lightning, and the wind is howling out there. But there were no signs of a tornado anywhere. The rain not only made it difficult to see, but the buildings made it extremely difficult to see if any tornado was coming.

Sawyer looks up from his phone, where he is glancing at the radar. "Guys, it looks like the tornado might be in Peterson according to the radar."

An emergency alert comes over the radio, warning us of a tornado. Outside, sirens are now going off.

"Okay, guys," Jonah says. "A tornado is here. Keep your eyes appeal for anything that could indicate it is near."

Lindy points to a gas station up ahead on our right. "Jonah, I'm going to pull into that gas station. There's no way we can chase this tornado if we can't see it coming. These buildings are making it difficult to see, and the rain is making it worse. I can't see the road. There are no open spaces where we can get a good look for the funnel. We can pull in here, keep watch where we can get a better view of the funnel approaching. If we need to, we can seek shelter inside."

Jonah nods. "I agree. As much as I want to chase this tornado, we are blind sighted right now. Pull into the gas station and we can get a good look at our surroundings. It's no good to chase it if we aren't able to see through the rain."

"We need to get to shelter soon," Sawyer says, his eyes still on his phone. "The hook echo is getting closer to us."

"Hang on, Sawyer," Lindy says. "We will pull in here and storm watch."

Jonah winds down his window. The rain blows in. The sirens were still blaring loudly. It's also really windy, the trees blowing to one side and there's this roaring sound from the wind. Jonah winds the window back up.

"It doesn't look good out there," he says. "The storm is getting worse. The tornado could be close."

Lindy slows, flicking on the indicator to turn right into the gas station. There's a couple of cars pulling into there, either to fill up their vehicles or they were seeking shelter from the storm.

Before Lindy is able to turn into the gas station, the lid of a trash can hits the bonnet of the car, and it is flown into the air again.

We sit there for a moment, not daring to move. Was the tornado close to us like Sawyer had said about the hook echo? Or was it just strong winds? We didn't have any visual on a funnel.

The street lights in front of us began to flicker. To our left, there's a spark of blue-green lighting, just behind the building we are near approximately one street away.

"Power flash!" Sawyer screams.

The tornado we were searching for is here. It's right next to us, about to cross in front of us. Lindy doesn't dare to move. The car behind us is honking at us to move, but there's a chance we might need to move backwards. But how could we when another vehicle is behind us? And it's quite possible it's too late to pull into the gas station to seek shelter. The tornado was already here.

Debris is now flying by, hitting our car. The vehicle behind us realizes what is happening, and reverses backwards. Lindy does the same as an unknown object hits the windshield, cracking it, getting us out of the danger path.

"We have debris!" Owen screams, filming everything.

Within seconds, the tornado is crossing the road right in front of us.

Chapter 16

Is this how Jeremy and his uncle felt when they realized the danger they were in? Were they aware they were close to the tornado? Were they in the circulation of it? Did they just make the wrong decision at the time?

These questions I may never know.

But perhaps it was like how it was for us right now.

Lindy has managed to move us backwards as soon as the car behind us moved also, away from the flying debris.

Someone is yelling, "We were almost in the tornado! We were almost inside it!"

But I have no idea who is saying it. Owen, I think.

The twister roars as it passes in front of us. Lightning flashes and the car's headlights capture the rotating column of air in front of us. Everyone in the car has a mixture of fear and excitement in their voices. I should share the excitement, but all I can think about is Jeremy.

Just seconds ago, we were right in the path of the tornado. If we hadn't spotted the debris or the power flashes, or the power hadn't been cut, we would have been doomed. Or if we hadn't stopped where we were, that would have been it.

The car shakes as the vortex passes us. Some debris is still hitting us even after we had moved backwards and was at a safe distance. The tornado moves fast across the road, destroying everything in its path. In the car everyone is practically peeing their pants, yet at the same time they are excitedly filming our encounter. Owen is saying how amazing this is. Over the roaring wind, the sirens continue to wail.

I sit there, grabbing the back of Sawyer's seat, holding onto it with my dear life. All I can think about is Jeremy and his last moments. I'm screaming inside my head that I cannot end up like Jeremy. I promise Avery I will make it home alive.

The tornado passes us in seconds. Everyone is talking at once, saying things like "Did you see that?" "I can't believe that!" "That was a close one!"

I unbuckle my seat belt, and then leap out of the car.

"Where are you going, Anna?" Jonah calls out to me.

"Stay in the car, Anna," Lindy calls out. "It's not safe out there."

I didn't listen. I ran out into the rain, running onto the road, careful not to get too close or put myself into more danger. I watch as the twister moves on after it tore up the gas station we were going to pull in just seconds ago. It was difficult to see, but the lightning was the only way I could see through the darkness.

The tornado didn't toss our car. It didn't toss it. I clench my fist to my side. How could it not have tossed our vehicle, but it tossed Jeremy's? It's not like I wanted it to pick up the car. We were so close to the funnel and near the circulation. Maybe we were just in the right spot so the wind couldn't pick us up. Jeremy and Chris, though, were unfortunate.

Wiping out the gas station where just minutes ago we had thought about taking shelter in, leaving it half standing, the twisting vortex keeps moving.

"Anna!" Jonah calls out to me once it was safe to get out of the vehicle.

He reaches me, putting a hand on my shoulder. I shrug him off, grabbing a small piece of wood from the road and hurl it in the air. Where it lands, I have no idea.

"Why did you take Jeremy?" I scream at the tornado as it moves further into the distance. Lightning and power flashes shows me where it is until I'm in complete darkness again. "Why didn't you take me too? You could have pick us up like you did to Jeremy!"

Of course, this tornado had nothing to do with Jeremy. But still, how did I get lucky and he didn't? Why was he the one to die?

I fall to my knees, not even sure what was on the ground in front of me. I cover my face and cry.

Jonah rests his hand on my shoulder. This time I don't shrug him off. He kneels down beside me.

"Hey, it's going to be okay, Anna," he assures me.

The doors of the car open and close behind me. "Anna, are you alright?" Sawyer asks.

I wipe my eyes and turn to look at the team. Lindy and Sawyer both have a torch in their hand, shining it in my direction. They look at me with concern, unsure how they could confront me. They see the devastation tornadoes leave every spring and summer, even in the non-storm season months. Sawyer and Owen may even have lost someone to a tornado. Lindy and Jonah have lost both Jeremy and their Uncle Chris in one.

"Why did Jeremy and Chris die when getting close to a tornado, but we didn't?" I ask.

The question hangs there for a minute, because how could you answer it? Tornadoes act in mysterious ways. Like it could destroy a whole neighorhood, but leave one building completely untouched.

Lindy answers, shrugging. "I can't give you the answers for that, Anna. Sometimes I wonder what happened that day just as much as you did. Both of them knew how to be safe, but maybe they were close and hadn't realized it, or maybe they were at a safe distance but the tornado shifted its path and they weren't aware until it was too late. We got lucky, I guess. If I didn't stop where we were, just an inch more we could have been toss."

"Owen and I don't know Chris or Jeremy," Sawyer speaks up. "But we can imagine what the three of you are going through with your loss, and how these chases seem difficult without them here. No one can explain what happen to them. Sometimes on chases everything is unpredictable. There are times when we can be caught off guard by the tornado, especially tonight. That's the danger of chasing at night. You can't see the tornado. We have done night chases a couple of times with another group of chasers. This was the first time during a night chase where we have gotten that close. Other times we have managed to keep a distance and spot it before we get too close."

"What happened to Chris and Jeremy was unfortunate," Owen adds. "Jonah and Lindy have told us stories of chases they have done with him, how Chris knew how to be safe when chasing so everyone is safe. That day he was killed; he could have gotten caught off guard and wasn't able to move out of the danger zone quick enough."

It made perfect sense to what the brothers had said. Chris has always made sure he didn't get close to a tornado to keep both Jeremy and me safe. Perhaps that's what happened that day. Chris was caught off guard and wasn't able to back up until it was too late.

Owen helps me off the ground. "Come on, Anna. Let's get back in the car."

Lindy shook her head. "No. Let's go and see if anyone needs help." She looks over at the gas station. "Oh gosh, the gas station is really wiped out. All of those people who took shelter…"

Her voice trails off.

Glancing around, the devastation of the tornado is terrible. It takes me back when I emerged from the bathroom at Avery's school. The devastation is so hard to describe because you're trying to get your head around it all. I don't even know where to start searching for people. Looking over to where some of the houses used to be, I wonder if people who could have been sleeping have made it down to their shelters or basements in time, if not the bathroom.

The first thing we did was search the houses. Using torches or our phones, we made our way over to the wreckage. We call out to people, moving debris and helping people who have trouble getting out from their shelters because debris was blocking the door. There were a few people who managed to get to shelters, and there were others who was completely off guard and didn't make it into the basement or the bathroom, stuck under debris.

Everywhere I look was damage. People wander around dazed, some don't even have shoes on and are careful to where they are treading. Around us there are emergency sirens or people calling out to others or are crying hysterically. My heart went out to them all and wished there was some way I could help rather than just searching the rubble and making sure people are okay.

It was probably too early to excess the damage, but it looked like maybe an EF2 or EF3.

Avery. I need to call him. I haven't had the chance to tonight, and I wanted him to know how I was. I decided when I call him that I wouldn't tell him about the tornado. I don't want him to freak out.

I pull out my phone to call my brother, but there was no signal on my phone. Maybe I will call him back at the motel later.

"Everything okay, Anna?"

I look up to see Lindy walking over to me.

I nod. "I'm okay."

"You were pretty upset before and I just wanted to make sure you are okay."

I give her a small smile. "I promise you I'm okay. I got a little emotional after the tornado passed in front of us."

"You know you are welcome to talk to me about Jeremy. He's my step-cousin, and it hasn't been easy with his death for the past few weeks. It hasn't been easy for Jonah and I to come out here to do storm chasing, but we force ourselves to do it. We didn't want their deaths to stop us from doing what we love."

"How do you come out here and chase after what happened to them? I'm finding it so hard to chase without Jeremy."

Lindy looks around at everything before turning back to me. "It's not easy, but we are doing it because it's something we both enjoy, and it helps us to study storms out in the field for our classes."

"Besides, Jeremy and Chris, have you lost someone in a tornado?"

She nods. "My grandmother died a few years ago. There was no warning and the tornado struck her house. Sometimes I wish I was there to help her to get to safety. That's why I study tornadoes. I want to understand them more, and figure out better warning systems. Something that could predict a tornado before it even forms. The tornado that killed her was rain wrapped. Even chasers weren't able to spot it and get the warning out."

"I'm sorry to hear that, Lindy."

She gives me a small smile. "You know, Anna, storm chasing is more than a job for me, or something I'm doing on the side of my meteorology degree. It's like a way of life that I must do every spring and summer. You see things you don't want to see, and sometimes we have family and friends who are in the path of it while we are on a chase. All we can do is hope they are safe. While we are out on the chases, we help the community."

I smile, thinking of what Jeremy loved about chasing. After the tornado strikes, we would help out anyone who needed help or could be trapped under the rubble. At one time, this woman had lost her dog, in which it went missing during the storm. Jeremy and I went searching for the dog and found it a couple of blocks away where the tornado hit.

But of course, not everything was good news. Sometimes we find dead bodies, and that's something we don't want to see. We help with the injure also, making sure people are okay.

I think about what Sawyer and Owen had said earlier to me, how chases are unpredictable. I guess for Jeremy and Chris's last chase, it was unpredictable. They didn't know they were going to die. Maybe the tornado shifted its track, catching them off guard before they knew they were in the wrong spot. I wish if I could go back to that day, I would have told Jeremy not to chase it. But knowing him, he probably would have. Tornadoes were his life. He would do anything to see one.

This is what Jeremy lived for. He lived for the thrills and adventures. During the aftermath, he's there helping anyone in need.

Maybe I storm chase for a whole different reason to Jeremy. I storm chase to capture the amazing cloud formation, lightning and the tornadoes. And being on this chase made me really understand why Jeremy did it. Not because he was inspired by the best tornado chasing movie of all time. No. He did it to study storms and to ensure people's safety. Even if I wanted to give it all up because it was something we did together, I couldn't do it. Like Moxie had said, Jeremy wouldn't want me to give it all up. Storm chasing was addictive. I could stop, but as soon as spring comes along and the storms start rolling around, I'm going to grab my camera. I couldn't wait for the storms to come to me. I had to get out there and chase them.

Chapter 17

After the rough night, helping locals, we head out the next morning. We chase for two more days, driving across Oklahoma, Texas and Arkansas. One storm we chased didn't produce any tornadoes, but I manage to get good shots of the storm.

The last storm we chase in Kansas didn't happen until sunset. A funnel cloud formed, the sky turning gold with a mixture of orange and yellow in the background of the storm. The funnel looked amazing with the backdrop. I have never experienced a tornado at sunset before and it was so beautiful. Jeremy would have loved this chase.

As I snap away, getting as many great shots as I could, I think about Jeremy. I don't want to think about how he isn't here. Instead, I think about how the times we chased together, and how much he would have loved chasing with his cousins and their friends.

This week has been great, even when I couldn't enjoy this moment with Jeremy. If we weren't friends, I probably would never have gotten into storm chasing. I would probably still do photography, but I wouldn't be a storm photographer. And if I wanted to give it all up because it wouldn't be the same without my best friend, this trip taught me that it's something I couldn't do. Like Moxie had said, Jeremy wouldn't want me to give it all up. Storm chasing with Jeremy has given me a chance to travel across the mid-west with his uncle, being able to capture and experience amazing storms. Maybe I'm not into the science side of it all like Jeremy, but I'm drawn to the beauty of them. Some people will say that Jeremy and I are insane, like Moxie would, but there is something about storms that has drawn us together.

And being out here with Jonah, Lindy and the twins has inspired me to know what I wanted to do with my life, even if this trip has been emotional for me. The four of them have been there with me and I'm thankful to be able to work with them.

Tomorrow, I'm heading home. There's a brief moment of sadness as I think about it, knowing Jeremy won't be next door. But I tell myself it's going to be okay. I talked to Mom the other night, and she said the Haydens were going to be staying in Brooke's Creek. For the mean time they are staying next door to us, but do plan to move to a small place in a few months. They just decided to wait until the town started to get back onto their feet. There are plans to start rebuilding the town in July. I'm just glad they won't be completely out of my life, and I will be able to see them every once in a while. The Haydens was a second family to me, and I don't know what I would do if they weren't around anymore.

Later that evening after returning to our motel, I sit with Lindy on my bed as we look through the photos I had taken this week. I haven't uploaded any new pictures onto my laptop yet since the second day chase. Lindy holds my camera as she flips through it. I also show her my Instagram feed.

"These pictures are fantastic," Lindy says, looking through my camera. "You have a great eye."

"Thanks."

She pauses on one photo, and stares at it for a minute before turning it towards me. It was one I had taken yesterday where I captured this stove pipe tornado at the right time with a rainbow behind it. The sunlight and rain seem to have appear at the right moment for me to get this shot. This was the rarest shot I have ever gotten of a twister. Jeremy would have loved this rare moment.

"I love this one," she tells me, handing the camera back to me. "It has to be my favorite shot. Do you think you can send me a copy?"

I take the camera. "Of course I can."

"Have you consider selling your shots? I reckon you could make some good money from it. I sell some of the footage I film on our chases. I'm lucky to get about $500 from them."

I shake my head, switching off the camera and put it back in the bag. "No. Never. Jeremy reckons I should."

"He's right. These photos are really good."

"Maybe someday I will. I guess I will decide what I want after college. I plan to have my own studio, but I haven't decided exactly what I will do. I don't think I want to take pictures of people. I like more of landscapes and storms."

Lindy smiles at me. "Well, whatever you decide to do, I would love to buy your prints. I hope to also see you on future chases."

Future chases. Looking back on these photos and thinking about the community we helped the other night, there's no way I wanted to stop. Next month Jonah and Lindy have invited me to go on the last chase of the season, the chase I was originally supposed to join them on with Chris and Jeremy.

There's still this fear I have when I see a tornado, taking me back to day when I hid in the bathroom. But the fear is brief when I see the photo potentials I could get. Going onto this chase and getting up close to the tornadoes was able to give me a new angle shot, to see how powerful the vortex is then when I'm shooting from a distance. Being on chases was different photographing thunderstorms in my backyard. Out here, there was this sense of freedom being out on the open road, chasing a storm that you never know what the sky will do. Each storm was different, a story to tell, and I wanted to capture it through the lens of my camera.

And I wouldn't be doing any of this without Jeremy.

Being out here with Jeremy's cousins and the twins has been an amazing experience. Even if I couldn't chase with my best friend, there are other chasing teams I could tag along with.

"I will definitely come along in the future," I tell Lindy.

Lindy smiles. "I'm glad. It has been great getting to know you, Anna. I didn't get to spend much time with you when you came to the wedding. I also wish we could have gotten a chance to go chasing together with Jeremy and Chris in the past."

I smile, thinking about how Jeremy would be like on this

trip. I just know he would get along well with everyone here. He would be talking non-stop about tornadoes. Chasing was his happy place. I imagine him writing a book someday, educating people on these deadly, but beautiful storms. English has never been his favorite subject, but I'm sure he would have written a book anyway, talking about his storm chases.

"I remember how weather was the only thing he would talk about," I say. "He hated school, and would often get into trouble for looking out the window. He would much rather be out chasing storms then sitting in a classroom."

Lindy laughs. "He reminds me of when I was little, beginning an interest in the weather. I wish I had known Jeremy longer, but I have only gotten to know him within the past two years since my mom started dating Jonah's dad. But I have enjoyed his company with the little time I have spent with him. You know, Anna, if you ever want to go chasing, you're welcome to join our team whenever we go out. I also chase with my boyfriend some days, so if you would like to come chasing with us, you're welcome to."

I smile. "I would like that, Lindy. Thanks."

There's a knock on our door. Lindy gets up and peeks out the window to see who it is. She unlocks the door, revealing Jonah on the other side.

"Hey, Jonah," she says. "What can I do for you?"

"I was wondering if I could borrow Anna for a second," he says.

Lindy moves aside for him. "You sure can."

Jonah steps into the room. "Hey, Anna. Are you busy?"

I shake my head. "No, not at all. Lindy and I were looking at the photos I had taken this week."

"Do you want to come outside?"

I follow him outside, and we headed over to the pool area. It was a nice night after an afternoon with storms. There were still some clouds about, the moon trying to peek through.

We sit down on the edge of the pool, dangling our feet in the water.

"What are you getting up to once you get back home?" Jonah asks me.

"One of the things I want to do is upload my photos onto my laptop," I answer. Honestly the photos will be a distraction from Jeremy. "What are you getting up to?"

"Well, I have exams next week."

"You have exams, and you spent a week chasing storms instead of being at school or studying?" I raise an eyebrow.

"I study meteorology online. I can't stand to be in a classroom, so in between chasing I do my online classes. The others don't study online. They don't have any class this week, so that's why we chose to go out chasing. But next week, we will be preparing for the exams."

"Well, I hope you all do well. Jeremy said it's your first year of college. How has it been so far?"

"It has been great. Are you looking forward to starting in the fall?"

"I'm looking forward to new experiences. I'm studying photography in the fall, perhaps start my own business someday."

"Awesome. I know you have had doubts about continuing to chase without Jeremy, but do you think you will keep on chasing? You make an excellent storm photographer."

I smile. I had a lot to think in the last few days of chasing, and I knew what I wanted to do. "I'm going to keep chasing. I love taking photos of storms, and I want to keep doing what

Jeremy and I enjoyed doing. My friend Moxie reckons if I stop, I wouldn't be happy. I most definitely will join you guys on a trip one last time before the season ends."

Jonah smiles brightly. "I have been hoping you would say that." He moves his hand over to mine that is resting on the edge of the pool, and places his hand over mine. "I really enjoyed chasing with you, Anna."

"I enjoyed it too, even on days when I felt down because Jeremy wasn't here with us."

"He would be proud of you, Anna. He would be proud of you for going out there even when you didn't think you could chase anymore."

I glance up at the sky. The moon was still hidden behind clouds, but it was trying its best to break through. There's some clearing where I can see stars twinkling brightly.

Jeremy would be proud I didn't stop chasing. And he would definitely be happy I'm chasing with his cousins. Chasing with them made me feel like I wasn't alone, that somehow, he was here still. There was something addictive about chasing tornadoes. The moment Jeremy and I first sat down to watch *Twister*, it opened a whole new world for us. When I first started getting into photography, the sky captivated me and it became something I enjoyed taking photos of. I was no meteorologist, but after this trip, I realize being a storm photographer is what I'm best at. There's a beauty side of a terrifying storm, and that's what I wanted to capture.

Epilogue

June 18ᵗʰ, 2022

Arriving home from the chase was hard at first. It was good to be home to see my family again. Moxie even came over to stay a few days with me. Her family had found a house to rent outside of Brooke's Creek, where they were unsure if they will live there permanently yet, or if they will move back to Brooke's Creek once everything is built again. It was hard to talk about my excitement about the week I had with people who weren't interested in chasing. But they listened and I'm thankful they did.

Jonah checked in on me every day, asking me how I was doing. I told him about the photos I had taken from a few thunderstorms that formed around Brooke's Creek. Mom even allowed me to borrow her car to drive out to get photos. I never went far. Just out on the highway to watch the storms roll in. Taking photos was helping me to take my mind off everything. My next storm chasing trip with Jonah and the others was the day after Jeremy's birthday.

The first time I had went outside of my town to watch a storm, I drive right past where Jeremy and Chris had died. No one knew the exact spot they were killed, but Chris' SUV was found nearby this road. It was hard to pull over at first, trying to hold back the tears as a lump formed in my throat. Mr. and Mrs. Hayden, possibly other family members, had come to this spot and had placed two crosses on the side of the road. Lindy and Jonah haven't come here yet, but they are making the trip to see my graduation before we go on the chase, and to stop by the memorial site to say goodbye to their cousin and uncle one last time. Their names were engraved on the crosses, and bouquet of flowers rest up in front of them. The flowers looked like they were placed there a few days ago with some of the petals browning and wilting. I wonder when these crosses were placed, and wished I was there when Jeremy's family had placed it. Perhaps it was only family who attended this memorial.

I didn't stay by the roadside memorial for long. Not when I'm alone. I didn't want to break down or still be out here when the storm hit.

Each day the hole in my chest was healing. Some days I wanted to run over to next door to talk to Jeremy, and then remember that he isn't here. There have also been times when I sat by my window at night as an evening storm rolls in, expecting he will sneak over at any moment to discuss the storm. Even with reports of tornadoes, I expected him to come on over to say "Let's go chase them!"

Avery was still pretty much scared whenever a storm rolls in the afternoon. He hides in the basement in the afternoons in case a tornado was to come, even if there's no warning for one. In the evenings he will come into my room. I cradle my brother in my arms as we sit by the window, watching the lightning and rain, telling him everything is going to be okay. I hope this fear of his will disappear eventually, although it can be hard to forget the sound of a roaring freight train. In my nightmares, I hear it.

On June 18th, Jeremy's birthday, where he would have turned eighteen, Moxie and I visit the cemetery. Avery tags along with us in his baseball uniform. I told him I wanted to stop by here before I take him to practice. There's already a fresh bouquet of flowers in front of his grave, as well as Chris, where family had stopped by earlier.

Avery places the bouquet I had brought, in which he wanted to hold for me, and place it down with the others.

Together the three of us stand there, holding hands in silence.

"You know, as much as I hated him obsessing over the weather, I miss him telling me about the storms we will get," Moxie says.

"I miss him coming over to help me practice baseball," Avery speaks up. "He hated sport, but whenever he came over to help Anna baby-sit me, he would get a glove and we would play catch."

I keep my eyes on Jeremy's grave, feeling both Moxie's and my brother's eyes on me, waiting for me to say something. My heart aches as I think about him.

"I miss being around him," I say, choking on my words as the tears began to fall. "I miss him being next door, and sharing his excitement about storms. But mostly, I miss being his storm chasing partner."

Avery let's go of my hand and wraps his arms around my waist. "It's okay, sis."

Moxie let's go of my hand and wraps an around my shoulders.

"It's going to be okay, Anna," Moxie assures me. She sniffs.

We stand there like this for a few minutes before I pull away to wipe my eyes. Moxie wipes her eyes as well.

"Bill Harding may be fictional, but I think he would be honored that Jeremy looked up at him," I say. "Chasing his dreams and being passionate towards storms. I can almost see Jeremy being great friends with him."

"I definitely see that as well."

I recall the memory when he first told me he wanted to be a storm chaser. How he wanted to get up close to study tornadoes. He lived his dream. Now I was going to continue through his, and live my own.

Acknowledgements

After writing *Chasing the Storm*, I was asked to write a sequel. I tried to, but a sequel just didn't work out even if I wanted it to. I did want to write another storm chasing story, though. It just took me a few years to come up with an idea for one. The storm chasing scenes were the hardest for me to write, especially when I have never seen a tornado or gone storm chasing, so there was a lot of watching documentaries and tornado movies, trying to visualise everything in my head.

I first got the idea for this story back in January 2020, just a few weeks before the pandemic started. It was the start of my writing slump, and I had no idea what I wanted for this story. The only thing that came to me was the prologue. It wasn't until January 2023 where I became inspired. Shortly after I started writing it, the sequel to *Twister* was announced, which became my motivation to write this story.

The movie *Twister* is a big inspiration to my character Jeremy. I first saw the movie when I was seven years old when it came out on VHS. Though I loved the movie, I was terrified of tornadoes. But over time, I grew a fascination towards them when watching documentaries. And when I learned that you could do storm chasing tours, it has been a bucket list thing for me to do some day. I watched *Twister* over and over again while writing this story, trying to understand my characters on what drew them to storm chasing after watching the movie. I'm still trying to figure it out for myself, but tornadoes just fascinate me. Like Anna, I'm not into the science side of storm chasing. Though I live in Australia, where we don't get many tornadoes as the US, I enjoy watching the clouds, especially when a storm is rolling in. Sometimes I like to photograph them myself, and I know if I ever do get a chance to storm chase one day, I would never get enough of photographing the sky.

To my favourite storm chaser who I really admire, Reed Timmer, your videos often helped me whenever I was writing the storm chasing scenes, and of course your favourite quote: "Never stop chasing" was a constant reminder to why my character Anna should keep chasing.

To my friends and family, along with my readers who follow me on social media, sorry that you had to put up with me chatting about this story where I constantly talked about tornadoes, whether I was telling you what I learned in a documentary or I was talking about *Twister*. Thank you for putting up with me on that, especially those who think I am crazy for wanting to storm chase. Maybe I am crazy, but I can't help wanting to do something I am so fascinated about.

Thank you to my editor Mindy, who was super excited about reading a manuscript about storm chasing. Without you, the story wouldn't be what it is.

Thank you also to who has picked up this book. Thank you for reading Anna's story, and may you also follow your dreams, to whatever you dream of chasing.

About the Author

Jessica Madden was born and raised in Sydney, Australia. She began writing stories since the age of eight. When she was nine, she realised that she wanted to be a writer more than anything in the world. At twenty-three years old, Jessica published her first book *Right Here Waiting for You.* Writing about characters falling in love has always been her favourite thing to write about.

When she is not writing, Jessica is often daydreaming up new storylines, and can be found lost in reading a good book.

You can follow her on Twitter and Instagram **@JessicaCMadden**

Also by Jessica Madden

Right Here Waiting for You
The Jet Lag Diaries
Silent Love
Chasing The Storm
If You Had Stayed
Hating Jamie Jackson
This Song Is for You (coming soon)

With You
One Whole Night with You
Every Moment with You

I Wasn't Supposed to Fall for You
I Wasn't Supposed to Fall for You
It's All Because Of You